F
LAN

Landrum, Graham

The Rotary Club
murder mystery

$17.95

THE ROTARY CLUB
MURDER MYSTERY

Also by Graham Landrum

The Famous DAR Murder Mystery

>> THE <<
ROTARY
CLUB
MURDER
MYSTERY

GRAHAM
LANDRUM

>> ST. MARTIN'S PRESS <<
NEW YORK

Design by Basha Zapatka

Library of Congress Cataloging-in-Publication Data

Landrum, Graham,
    The Rotary Club murder mystery / Graham Landrum.
        p.   cm.
    "A Thomas Dunne book."
    ISBN 0-312-09375-6
    1. Women detectives—Tennessee—Fiction.   I. Title.
PS3562.A4775R6   1993
813'.54—dc20   93-4110
                                                     CIP

First edition: August 1993

10 9 8 7 6 5 4 3 2 1

THE ROTARY CLUB
MURDER MYSTERY

THE DAY IT BEGAN

>> *Henry Delaporte* <<

Although the Rotary mystery is by no means so famous as the Famous DAR Murder Mystery, it has many things in common with that investigation and is in some ways more remarkable.

Both crimes took place in Borderville, Virginia-Tennessee, and the identities of both murderers were ferreted out by Mrs. L. Q. C. Lamar Bushrow. In each case, a chapter of a nationally important organization was involved, and in each case the nature of the crime was initially misunderstood.

The second case is more remarkable than the first because, among other things, Mrs. Bushrow is now two years older than she was when she solved the DAR mystery. The DAR mystery was clarified to some degree by coincidence, but the Rotary mystery was explained largely through logical processes backed up by patient detective work on the part of Mrs. Bushrow.

By all that is right and proper, I ought not to have anything to do with the telling of this story, but Mrs. Bushrow, who furnished the public such a charming account of her activities in *The Famous DAR Murder Mystery,* absolutely refused to put pen to paper unless I agreed to referee the book in somewhat the same way that Mrs. Parsons presided over the DAR account.

I am, of course, happy to accede to Mrs. Bushrow's request, for two reasons. On the one hand, her refusal to record her activities in this case would deprive the public of the pleasure of continued acquaintance with her. And on the other, my personality as my wife depicted it in the former book was not altogether as I would like the public to think of me. You will find that a wife's-eye view of a husband is often skewed, and I suppose that the observation of character at the close range of marriage can blur the image in the same way that the observation of a painting at too short a distance can interfere with our impression of the picture as a whole. Let us hope that I am not nearly so sententious as I appear from the references Helen— i.e., my wife—made to me in her share of *The Famous DAR Murder Mystery.*

As Professor Landrum pointed out in the preface to that book, the crime described had already taken place before the story began. Such was essentially the case with the murder presently under consideration. It occurred at the Borderville Motor Inn, universally referred to by Bordervillians as "the Inn," on May 26 or 27 last, at some time between 11:30 P.M. Monday and 2:00 A.M. Tuesday. But we were unaware of the fact until a little after noon on Tuesday.

Tuesday is Rotary day in Borderville. Helen calls it Sacred Tuesday because she says Rotarians are far more conscientious about Rotary than they are about church. She may be right about that; but as far as our club goes, we are neither very holy about church nor very careful about the attendance rules of Rotary. Our club, to our shame, has an attendance average of about 67 percent, for which we are constantly being chided by our sergeant at arms.

Nevertheless, there are some of us who are markedly constant in attendance, and I suppose I am one of them. I rarely miss unless I am out of town. I should, of course, make up my absence by attending another club, but it is often inconvenient or impossible to do so. The fact that I always attend when I am here in Borderville is due not to the excellence of the food or the interest stimulated by the programs, neither of which would be worth the quarterly dues of the club, but to my pleasure in the association I have with four men, who nearly always sit with me at the same table, up front, just to the left of the speaker.

Sitting there at the same table week after week is hardly in line with the ideals of the organization. But for those of us who are fifty and up, it is very pleasant to luxuriate in a familiar groove (a word of excellent connotation in my youth); and we, as "old boys," enjoy our own rather predictable conversation. Since there are six chairs at each table, we do not feel that we are exclusive, for anyone who wishes to sit with us is cordially welcomed to do so.

But the four regulars with whom I always eat are Trajan McDowell, Steve Johnson, Raymond Rogers, and Dr. Fred Middleton. We usually try to get to the Borderville Inn at five or ten minutes of twelve in order to pick up our food from the steam table and be seated before the rest of the club has arrived. By that means, we get the waitress to come directly to our table and thereby fill our cups immediately. Then, when she had poured coffee for all the rest, she comes back to us so that we always have coffee at hand to enjoy as we listen to the day's speaker.

Which is very important. That is to say, the coffee is very important.

Also important is the fact that the four men whom I have mentioned are all Presbyterians, three of them being elders in the First Presbyterian Church and the other a deacon in the Second Presbyterian Church. As the son of a Presbyterian minister, I joined the Episcopal church when I married, but there's something about being with men who grew up the way I did that is like going home. Whatever the reason for it, we form a very congenial group.

On that Tuesday, as usual, I arrived at the Inn about ten minutes before the appointed time. Because it had been announced that the district governor was going to speak to us, there were already quite a few Rotarians present.

Rotary district governors are in some ways pretty much the same. They are jolly men and always supportive, optimistic, and entirely sold on Rotary. They would have to be of that sort in order to spend the time, effort, and money required of a district governor. You see, a district governor, in addition to other duties, must visit each club in his district at least once a year. The result is that for a whole year, a district governor is called away from his business repeatedly; and unless he is retired or reasonably well fixed financially, there is an element of sacrifice in the governorship that a good many Rotarians would find difficult to afford. District governors, therefore, are on the whole financially successful as well as superior in other regards.

Do not think, however, that we look forward to the district governor's visit with enthusiasm. What the poor man has to say to us is pretty much what the former district governor said to us on a similar occasion the year before. The governor will always recite the praises of Rotary International, and these are certainly impressive. But when you have heard them for a quarter of a century, your mind is likely to wander somewhere between the Four-Way Test and the Paul Harris Fellowship. On the other hand, the district governor usually has three or four pretty good jokes.

But a local club, especially one like ours, which doesn't have a good attendance record, always tries to get all its members out for the district governor's visit. For a whole month before the event, the sergeant at arms reminds us of the impending honor, and our president assures us that we would not wish to be absent on such an important occasion. All in all, there is a great deal more bustle than usual about the meeting when the district governor is to be present.

As I say, I got to the Borderville Inn ten minutes early. Mabel Mahaffey was setting up her music on the spinet piano in the corner behind the flag. Joseph D. (Jody) Russell, our secretary-treasurer, was buzzing about doing the things he does. Warren Perkins was hanging the Rotary banners, four of them, on the wall behind the lectern. It was our typical, cheerful confusion.

Steve Johnson was already at the table. We had roast pork in honor of the district governor, and I noticed that Steve had helped himself rather generously to the meat. Then Trajan came in, got his plate, and sat down. Just about the time that Mrs. Mahaffey began to play, Raymond came in.

Steve began to tell us about some trouble the congregation at Second Presbyterian is having with its minister.

By that time, the room was pretty full and the noise level was so high that we could hardly hear Mrs. Mahaffey tinkling away at "Time on My Hands." The younger Rotarians don't care for the old songs, but the older fellows crave something they know—something that has a tune.

Ray has a new boat and told us about the fish he had caught on the preceding weekend. Steve wanted to know when Ray was going to take the rest of us out on the lake. And there was other chatter of the same sort, all inconsequential and very much the same conversation we had heard every Tuesday for twenty-odd years.

I looked down at my watch. It was 12:15. I realized that our president, Eugene Spencer, had been coming in and out and stirring around in a generally nervous way. But I supposed the district governor was getting to town a little later than expected.

Steve Johnson turned to Tom Shaefer at the next table and said, "The governor must have had trouble on that detour on Four twenty-one."

"Oh, the governor got in last night," Tom said. "He's staying here at the inn."

With that settled, we went on swapping stories and making comments for another ten minutes, when suddenly Eugene rushed in, his face very serious and white. He went immediately to the podium and, grasping the microphone, said, "Fellow Rotarians, something terrible has happened to the district governor. I have just been in his room. The police are here, and the sheriff is expected any minute. We will dispense with the program today. Go on eating."

Then he turned to Joe and added, "Take over for me, will you? I've got to go back over there. And you might get Art Stoneman to dismiss the club at the end with a prayer."

Silence fell on us. What were we to think? If the police and the sheriff were involved, was it murder?

From the back of the room, Keith Duncan—it would be Keith!—called out, "Come on, Gene, give. What happened?"

We all found our tongues at once.

"Yeah, tell us."

"What happened, Gene?"

"Come on, tell us."

And so on.

"I'd rather not just now," Gene answered. He was already halfway to the door. "Maybe later." And with that, he was gone.

Three or four of the men got up and followed. But the rest of us returned to our roast pork and bread pudding. The reverence soon wore off, and we were saying things like "Would you call this 'dead on arrival'?" and "We've had deadly district governors, but this is the first one who was actually dead."

Dreadful things to say—just dreadful!

And then Fred Middleton came in. He had most of the answers to what we wanted to know.

I therefore turn the story over to him.

THE SCENE OF THE CRIME

>> Frederick M. Middleton, M.D. <<

I was delayed at the office and did not arrive at the Borderville Inn until about ten minutes after twelve. I parked in the upper parking lot, the lower lot being full by that time. In consequence, I had farther to walk and was delayed still more.

The Inn is built in the form of a C around a swimming pool. The west side of the enclosure can be entered through an opening between two of the wings. As I came through this opening, I realized that something unusual was going on.

In front of one of the first-floor rooms halfway to the Inn office stood Gene Spencer, Nancy Attwood (manager of the motel), and a young fellow in a blue blazer with the Inn monogram on the breast pocket. I was in time to hear Nancy say, "Go ahead, Jim. Break the door open."

With that, the young fellow lunged with his shoulder at the door, but nothing happened. He took another try at it, and I heard wood splintering.

By that time, I was close enough to see that the door had been on the chain and that Jim had merely hit the door hard enough to jerk the chain from the doorjamb.

Mrs. Attwood entered the darkened room, turned on the

light, and immediately exclaimed, "Dear God!" Gene Spencer followed her and drew in his breath suddenly and audibly. I trailed young Jim into the room and saw lying composedly on the bed the body of a man about forty-five years old.

Gene Spencer, looking around, saw me and said, "Thank God! Here's a doctor."

I stepped past Gene and examined the figure on the bed. There was a small entry wound below the chin. The bullet had passed upward and blasted quite a hole in the cranium. Blood and brains were spattered about, and it appeared that the bullet was imbedded in the headboard. Near the man's right hand, I saw a service .45 automatic.

"I am of no use here, Gene," I said. "Only the undertaker can do anything for this man."

"My God!" Gene moaned, "It's the district governor!" The dead man was Charles Hollonbrook, who was to have addressed our club that very day.

"How long," Gene asked, "how long since it happened?"

The air conditioner was on and would have had an undue effect on the body. I am no coroner, but I made a guess.

"I would think it happened about the middle of the night."

Gene was visibly horrified. He had his hand up rubbing his forehead and kept saying, "Suicide! Suicide!" under his breath.

To discover any suicide is a great shock, but for the president of a Rotary Club to find that his district governor, who was about to address the club with a speech designed to inspire confidence and ring the changes on the glories of Rotary, had taken his life not a hundred feet from the dining room where the club was now assembled—that was indeed a blow.

"It certainly appears to be suicide," I said, "but let's look around and see what we find."

The room seemed to be in perfect order. Hollonbrook's glasses were on the bedside commode table and next to them was a small bottle. Aware that the police would undoubtedly look for fingerprints, I carefully picked up the bottle with my handkerchief—it was a popular brand of sleeping pills. I unscrewed the lid and saw that there were three tablets left. That, of course, did not indicate how many had been taken, since I did not know how many pills had been in the bottle when Hollonbrook checked in at the motel. The coroner would have to tell us whether any pills had been taken. Could the pills have been brought along as an alternate means of suicide? I did not think so. I felt that all the tablets would have been taken if suicide had been intended—or, alternately, the bottle would be full if the pills had been intended as a second option.

Under the bottle was a square of paper of the sort found in desk pads. Across the top of the page was printed: "From the Desk of Charles Hollonbrook." On the paper was scrawled: "Sorry to disappoint you, but I can't make it today, C.J.H."

I directed Gene's attention to the note.

Mrs. Attwood said, "I'm calling the police," and picked up the phone before I could warn her about fingerprints. But whether we were concerned with murder or suicide, it was unlikely that a call would recently have been made from that phone by anyone but Hollonbrook.

While Mrs. Attwood was calling, I said to Gene, "I think we should not necessarily conclude that this is suicide. The determination is for the coroner and the police to make." Of course, it certainly looked like suicide from the nature of the wound, the proximity of the gun, and the note. Nevertheless, it seemed strange that a man would jot a suicide note on a sheet from the desk pad in his office instead of writing it properly on Inn stationery conveniently available in the room.

As Mrs. Attwood had taken up the phone, she had knocked a book off the table. When I reached down and picked the volume up to replace it where it had been, I saw that it was *Break In,* a Dick Francis novel, with a bookmark inserted two-thirds of the way through it.

Gene kept repeating, "Suicide! Suicide!" as though he had not heard me.

About that time, I looked around and saw the young fellow who had broken the door in. He was in difficulties, face pale and eyes large. It was obviously the first time he had seen a corpse anywhere but at a funeral home.

"I guess we should stay here until the police come," I said.

"Yes!" Mrs. Attwood said in a rather firm voice. In spite of her apparent self-possession, she was pretty well shaken by the event. I believe that there had never been a violent death at the Inn before. This would not be good publicity for the motel. So it was an especially rough experience for her.

"Maybe we should look around further," I said.

The Borderville Motor Inn was built some time ago, when it was customary to enter the rooms from an outside walkway. The room has but the one entrance, and the remainder of the exterior wall is a plate-glass window, heavily draped and incapable of being opened. The room measures some twenty-five by fifteen feet. It contains a shag carpet and two beds, with the commode table between them. On the opposite wall is a low chest with a platform to hold luggage.

At the rear, there is a closet to the right and a door at the left, which opens on a small compartment containing the bath and toilet. Between the two, there is a counter into which a basin is fitted. There is absolutely no means of entering the room except through the door at the front. In the ceiling above the basin in this particular room, there is a square that looked as though it might be removed—no doubt to provide access to wiring or perhaps plumbing. But since there are rooms on the second floor of the motel, obviously there would be no way of entering the lower room through that square.

I did not see how anyone could have gotten in without waking the sleeper, could have then killed him, could have gotten out of the room, and could have secured the chain. It had to be suicide—obviously. But on the face of it, two things immediately seemed wrong to me: The note was one thing, but the other was altogether wrong. Nobody ever committed suicide when he had read only part of a Dick Francis novel.

I looked at the deceased's clothing: his suit neatly hung ready to put on, his shoes beautifully polished and carefully placed below the suit, his shaving equipment, placed on the counter ready to use, along with his toothpaste and toothbrush. It certainly looked as though the man who had gone to bed had expected to get up in the morning.

I went back to the center of the room. On the lowboy was a traveling clock ticking very quietly. I picked it up (with my handkerchief, of course). It had been set to go off at 7:30 and undoubtedly had done so.

Just then the patrolman came. After Mrs. Attwood explained what had happened and each of us had been identified, Gene told the policeman that he needed to say something by way of explanation to the club; and the officer permitted Gene and me to leave but instructed us to return and be questioned by the sheriff, who was expected momentarily.

Coming into the dining room as late as I did, I found the food on the steam table meager and thoroughly picked over. However, I got a sliver of the roast pork, a little more than a spoonful of English peas, and a quarter of a tomato by way of salad.

When I joined the boys at the front table, they were greatly excited over what had happened, as were the men at the other tables. I reported what I knew. All told, I doubt that any former district governor has provided us with as interesting a meeting as the one we had on that Tuesday. On the other hand, the interest of that day was nothing compared with the consternation when the truth about our district governor came out a number of weeks later.

When I had finished my lunch, I went back upstairs and found that the sheriff had arrived. Having appointments scheduled throughout the afternoon, I persuaded him to hear my evidence first so that I could go about my business.

The following morning I read this story in the *Banner-Democrat:*

SUICIDE AT LOCAL MOTEL

Police were called at 12:15 Tuesday to investigate the circumstances of the death of a guest at the Borderville Motor Inn.

The victim was a white male approximately forty years of age. He was found in bed, apparently a suicide.

Personnel at the Inn had no inkling that anything was amiss until approximately 11:40 a.m., when Eugene Spencer, 628 Dominion Terrace, attempted to reach the deceased by phone.

After several unsuccessful attempts, Spencer notified Inn Manager Nancy Attwood that further efforts to rouse the guest should be made. Attwood and attendant James R. Rickets, 1392 Linden Way, forced the door.

The victim was lying in bed, a bullet through his brain.

Sheriff R. M. Bowser informed the *Banner-Democrat* that the dead man had shot himself with a .45 automatic pistol. He said also that a suicide note was found beside the body.

The name of the victim is being withheld until his next of kin can be found and notified.

It should surprise no one that I was well enough pleased to have been left out of this account. But I received a call from the *Banner-Democrat* on Thursday afternoon, and I appeared in a minor way in the story that they carried on Friday morning.

By that time, Hollonbrook's wife had been located and informed, the reporter had ascertained the biographical facts about Hollonbrook, and Bowser had released the information that the automatic had been identified as Hollonbrook's property, which seemed to lend weight to the official contention that the death was suicide.

Pictures accompanied this story, including a shot of the chain that had been jerked loose from the doorjamb in order for motel staff to break into the room.

It seemed very obvious that this mechanism, once in place, would prevent admission from the outside without the cooperation of Hollonbrook. The fact that this mechanism was indeed in place and that the door was also locked in the conventional manner seemed to prove beyond possible doubt that Hollonbrook's death was suicide.

So in spite of the fact that I could not reconcile the note from Hollonbrook's desk pad and the unread portion of the Dick Francis book, and the obvious preparations he had made for the normal activities of the following morning, I certainly could not explain the death otherwise than as a suicide.

But I could not rid my mind of the suspicion that, in this case, suicide was the wrong verdict.

DEALING WITH MURDER AGAIN

>> Harriet Bushrow <<

The Rotary Club has always been gracious and attentive to the Rotary Anns—that's the wives and widows of Rotarians. Now that they have women in Rotary, I just wonder how that is going to be in future years.

As I say, until now the boys have always had a "Ladies' Night" once a year, honoring us wives and widows of Rotarians. And how they have always handed us around!—as though we were something precious. A lot of it was just put-on—the toast to the ladies and the ladies' response, and the corsages and dinner favors—but we loved it just the same. Now with women's lib and equal opportunity, I don't suppose the boys will want to honor us in the old way. Can they honor the Rotary Anns without honoring the Rotary Andies? And will they provide corsages for the widowers the same way they have always done for the widows?

But that's completely off the subject. What I started to say was that Rotary was always a big part of social life for me and Lamar. Lamar went into Rotary when he was thirty-five and remained in it until he died thirty-two years later. And during that time, some of the dearest friends we ever had were Rotarians and Rotary Anns.

The point is that many of the Rotarians were just as much friends when they were away from the Rotary meeting as they were when they were eating together at noon on Tuesday. And that's why Rotary meant so much to me.

We always had good times with Rotary friends and their wives. Often we would go on vacations with people we got to know through Rotary. But the thing that meant most to me then and does so still is the Rotary Bridge Club.

Of course, it never was a formal club at all. It started as just three tables of bridge, meeting twice a month; and we had more fun! It just happened that most of us were Presbyterians, and so, of course, we knew each other through the church as well as through Rotary.

But it was a long time ago that we had three tables of players. One by one, we have been passing over to the other side. But you know, the rest of us always saw to it that the widow or the widower had a way to continue to play with us. Sometimes we invited a new player to make up the number. And one year, two couples moved away to Florida about the same time.

What I am getting at is that there is only one table left. It is made up of me, Lona Champion, and Daisy Beth and Fred Middleton. So we are three Rotary Anns and Fred.

As you have already found out, the district governor died in the night between Monday and Tuesday, May 26/27. Then it was all in the paper on Wednesday and Friday. And then the Rotary Bridge Club met with Daisy Beth and Fred on Friday night.

Now do you think we did much serious playing that night? Oh yes, we bid and we made or did not make our bids, but our minds were altogether on one thing—and that didn't have much to do with the game.

Lona was having the time of her life because we were right there with Fred, and Fred had been on the spot even before the police arrived, and he was telling us all about it. I have to admit I was just as excited as Lona was—like the old fire horse smelling smoke.

Well, we talked it over and talked it over. And Fred made the observation that if the chain had not been on the door and the door had not been locked, he would seriously doubt that it was suicide. He didn't think the note sounded like evidence of suicide, and the poor man hadn't even finished his Dick Francis book.

"Of course it wasn't suicide," I said.

"Why do you say that?" Lona wanted to know.

"Well," I said, "you know very well that the dearest wish of every Rotarian in the country or maybe in the world is to be district governor. Not one of them would forgo being district governor even to go to Heaven—or Hell, for that matter. They love the idea of being district governor, and you know they do."

Lona thought maybe that was right, and Fred kind of chuckled, but he didn't say I was wrong.

"And as for that locked room," I went on, "I wouldn't let a thing like that stop me from calling it murder."

"You wouldn't?" Fred raised his eyebrows.

Ever since I cracked (notice the professional language!) the Famous DAR Murder Case, people pay attention to me when I talk about crime.

"No, I would not."

"You think a murder can take place in a locked room?"

"Locked room?" I said. "There is no such thing as a murder taking place in a locked room. The room was unlocked when the murder took place and then locked afterward."

"What are you going to do about that chain on the door?"

Well, I didn't know the answer to that one, but I wasn't about to admit it. Still, if it was murder, it had to have been done by somebody who got out of that room. And if that somebody figured out how to do it, it stood to reason somebody else could figure it out, too.

So we argued about that for a little. Then Daisy Beth said, "I understand that they couldn't find his wife for two days."

"Where did you hear that?" Lona was quick to ask.

"At the beauty parlor."

Beauty parlor information can sometimes be pretty accurate. And if what Daisy Beth had just said was true, that would explain why the *Banner-Democrat* had not run the second story until the third day.

"Well, it looks like we have a real mystery on our hands," Lona said. "And if anybody can find out just what happened, Harriet can."

Then Daisy Beth said, "Oh, Harriet, you just must do it."

I knew then that I should have kept my mouth shut, but I never was one to be quiet.

Fred was in rare form—went on quite a while teasing me the way he does. But pretty soon, he got just as serious as could be and said, "Would you really take the case?"

Well, just because I happened to figure out who killed that Mr. Garcia in the DAR Mystery, nobody needs to suppose I am a real detective. I am eighty-eight years old. Most folks think I am just an inquisitive old woman, and they may be right.

Fred would have none of that. He said, "Don't knock yourself. I have more confidence in your intelligence than I have in all the police in Virginia or Tennessee."

Now wasn't that sweet of him!

Then all of them began to get at me about looking into the case to see if I could solve it.

"Well, you know there's not much that a nosy old woman can't find out if she just keeps asking questions long enough," I said. And I must say that I'm pretty good at asking questions.

Fred became a bit reflective and said, "I honestly think there is something fishy about that suicide. I think the club ought to look into it. And, Harriet, I think you are the ideal person to do the snooping."

Then Lona and Daisy Beth got into it and said it would be the very thing to do.

I had no idea anything would come of it. But with my big mouth, I said I bet a woman could find the culprit sooner than a man could. It was just in fun, and I didn't mean a bit of it. Even though I worked out that DAR Mystery, that was the kind of thing that would happen just once in a lifetime.

But the more I carried on, the more I thought Fred was really serious. And yet you know how it is with things that are talked about over the bridge table—nothing ever comes of them. So I thought very little about Hollonbrook and all that until Sunday morning at church, when Fred Middleton came up to me and said, "Harriet, get your detective kit ready and start working on that case."

"What are you talking about?" I said. "Don't you know I would have to go to that town in North Carolina where that poor man came from?" But then I thought—and smiled. "You know one of my dearest friends lives in that town. If you'll pay my way down there, I promise you I'll sleuth till the cows come home." Then I laughed and said, "I'll send *you* the bill, Fred Middleton."

"It's a deal." Fred smiled. "We have already put together ten Rotarians who are willing to take care of the expenses if you'll lend us your brain."

Now that was just ridiculous. Of course, there was the DAR Mystery, but I had no idea of ever doing such a thing again. Besides, everything about the DAR case took place right here in Borderville, and that meant that Margaret and Lizzie and Helen, three other ladies in our DAR chapter, were all working on it. And then Helen had those contacts on the West Coast. So it wasn't as if I solved the mystery by myself.

But this case was bound to be different. You see there wasn't anybody around here that knew this Mr. Hollonbrook at all. And that seemed to say that the answer was all down there in North Carolina. I just didn't know whether I could do it.

But here they were offering to pay my expenses!

I said, "Fred, you rascal, what have you gotten me into?"

"But you are going to do it," he said.

I said, "I'll have to think about it." And then I walked off and left him.

Well, the more I thought about it, the more excited I was. And so I got up on Monday morning and put on my white dress with the big black polka dots and my white straw hat with the red poppies on it and my red kid shoes. I can't wear high heels anymore. My bunions won't allow it. But these are real nice shoes with heels about an inch high. And of course I wore my cut crystal beads—the same ones that I had to break to solve the DAR murder. But that sweet Helen Delaporte! She took the beads to Reinhold's Jewelers and had them sent to someplace in New Jersey where they strung them professionally.

There's nothing in the world I would take for those beads, because that darling Lamar gave them to me when we were married.

After I got myself all fixed up, I called Fred Middleton at his office. He's seventy-three, but he still practices. I said, "Fred, give me the number of that room where that man was killed at the motel." It was 106. Then I got into my old DeSoto and drove over to the Borderville Motor Inn to have breakfast.

It is a right nice place. The folks are friendly and the food is good, even if it is a bit expensive. But breakfast is the reasonable meal, and that was part of the reason why I wanted to have a late breakfast there. You'll find out the rest of the reason in just a minute.

There was a nice head-in parking place in front of the Inn when I drove up just after 9:30. I rolled up the car window, locked the door, and walked to the entrance. Then I went in and stood there by the sign that tells you to wait for the hostess. When that young lady came, I asked her if they were serving on the deck by the pool.

The deck is just by the dining room, with a door right there, and it is so pleasant to eat outside in good weather. It is very pretty and nice, with round iron tables and those big umbrellas that come out of the middle.

"Why yes," she said, "if you'll just come this way."

Now I had to be seated out there on the deck so I could see room 106, the room where this Hollonbrook was killed.

I sat down on the nice rattan chair and put my red purse on the table, where I wouldn't forget it.

The young woman came out and took my order. I decided to have orange juice, a waffle, bacon, one egg over easy, and coffee. It came to $3.50 and was more breakfast than I usually eat, but it was already so late in the morning that I could count that as part of my lunch and just eat a bowl of cereal or something at noon.

There was hardly anyone around—just the one lady in her bathing suit, lying on a chaise longue on the other side of the pool. But she had a book and wasn't paying any attention to me.

It was cool and pleasant enough as I sat there munching my waffle. The hostess had been nice enough to switch on the outdoor Muzak machine, and it was playing some nice, soft music. So I was just having an elegant time when I saw what I was waiting for.

You see, the motel part of the building goes right around that pool on two sides, with the office and dining room forming the third side. Where the two rows of rooms come together at the corner, there is a place where you can come through.

I had just finished my egg when the maid came along the walkway, pulling a cart with a vacuum sweeper and a big hamper on it through that opening. She was a little meager sort of white woman in a uniform that was attractive enough, but it just drooped on her.

I watched her drag that hamper up to the first door on the other side of the pool. Then she picked up a key hooked to a wooden paddle about a foot long that she had hanging over the side of the hamper. She opened the door, wedged it open with a piece of wood, and then laid the key and the paddle over the edge of the hamper again.

She went inside, and in just a second the TV in that room began to blare out. Then she brought out a big pile of sheets and towels, dumped them into the hamper, and took the sweeper into the room. She pulled open the curtains and started vacking the rug.

And that was why she had turned up the TV so loud—so she could hear it above the racket of that sweeper. And it was loud, I tell you. Why, I heard it clear as day across the pool and above the Muzak!

According to my watch, it took her a little over ten minutes to run the sweeper, make the bed, and put out the towels. Then she closed the curtains, turned off the TV, dumped the soiled linen in her hamper, took the wedge out of the door so it would close, and went on to the next room, where she went through the same thing.

I noticed that every time she went into the rooms on that side of the pool, she would leave the cart with the hamper outside, right there in front of the window of the same room where she was working. That meant she could easily see everybody that might come along and stand anywhere near that cart.

But you see, if she got to the end of that row and then pulled her cart back to the corner where the two wings of the building came together, she would be starting out differently on that row because the first door she would come to would be right at the corner. So when she went to the next room, she would most likely drag the cart behind her and leave it in front of the window of the room she had already cleaned. And that was what I wanted to see her do.

So I just waited. I had three cups of coffee. I was almost embarrassed from being there so long, and it takes a lot to embarrass me. But finally, she got to the end of that row of rooms. And sure enough, she did just what I thought she would.

I paid my bill at the desk in the dining room and went on out the front door. Then instead of getting into my car and driving home, I turned to the left and walked down to the corner of the building and came all the way up the outside to that passage between the two wings of the motel. I just stood there until the maid had gotten to room 106. I could tell when she went from one room to another by the way the TV would be shut off. So I knew the minute when it was right for me to come out.

Sure enough, there was the cart parked outside the door of 106, but it was in front of room 107, in a position where I could easily have gotten hold of that key without being seen from 106. There was not a soul around except the lady in the bathing suit, and her chaise longue was positioned so that I was completely out of her sight.

Well I stood there for three minutes by my watch, which was plenty of time to take an impression of the key—in a bar of soap or a ball of wax—I think that's the way they always do it in detective stories. So that was one way someone could have gotten the key. But it would be risky—because if you were seen doing it, that would just let the cat out of the bag. Still, there might be other ways to get the key.

Then I heard the TV in room 106 go off, which meant that the little cleaning woman would come out.

I put on a big smile and said, "Good morning! Isn't this a perfect day! I was just standing here looking at that beautiful pool with the lovely blue water and all the bright colors of the umbrellas and the pretty furniture around."

She gave me a look as if to say, What is that old bat talking about?

"Have you worked here long?" I asked. Anything to get a conversation started!

" 'Bout five years."

"I bet you never had as much excitement as you did last week."

"Lord, no!" she said. "And I hope I don't never have nothing like it again. I come around here about nine, nine-thirty and knocked on that ther' door, see. Didn't nobody answer, so I thought it musta been empty an' unlocked it. But then I seen it was on that chain thang. So I jist said, ' 'Scuse me,' and went on to the next room, not thinkin' a'tall how that ther' man was a laying in ther' a corpse.

"See, I go off work when I get through all these here rooms. So I warn't here when they broke that ther' chain and found that pore soul a laying thar in his blood.

"Lord, Lord! That ther' piller was jist soaked in it."

My informant's voice became awed. "Ther' was parts of his brains in hit, too." She tilted her head back and a knowing look came into her eyes. "Hit was this here room, an' while I don't mind so much going in and doin' around in the daylight, I pities the pore folks that has to sleep in thar."

"I don't suppose they would know," I suggested.

"An' a blesset thang it'd be, ma'am."

"Could I just peek in and see it?" Oh, I sounded very timid when I said that.

The woman was as full of pride as if she were showing off her first grandchild. She almost bowed me into the room.

"Did you see the body?" I asked.

"Lord, no! I reckon I woulda been skeered to death. But I know wher' he was a layin', fer I taken the sheets and the piller and all that offen the bed. There was some blood got on that ther' mattress, but Miz Attwood said it warn't bad enough to have to change the mattress, 'cause folks wouldn't know." Suddenly, my informant put her hand over her mouth. "I ain't suppos' to talk about hit," she mumbled.

I assured her that I certainly would not repeat anything she had said—and here I have given it word for word! You just can't trust an old woman.

I took a good look around while I had the chance. They had not put back the door chain. But I could see how the screws that had attached it to the door and the doorjamb had been pulled out and splintered the wood. That chain struck me as being the real problem. I could figure out ways to get the key, but what good would that do if the murderer couldn't put the chain on the door from the outside?

"I seen my granny die," the woman said. "An' I was thar when my man died, but I ain't never seen nobody that kilt their self before. Hit's skeery, I tell ye. Hit's all right in the daytime, but hit's skeery at night."

"I know what you mean," I said sympathetically. "I *do* appreciate your letting me see the room. Now you take care of yourself."

I suppose some of my readers might think I should have given the woman a tip. But she is one of our mountain women and, aware that she is every bit as good as I am, she would have been offended if I had offered. So I simply took myself off.

It gave me a lot to think about. There is, of course, as I have already observed, no such thing as a locked-room murder mystery. That door has to be open for the murderer to get in and to get out again. Even though there might be several ways a murderer could get in, I did not see how anybody could get out again and put that chain thing on the door.

I did not believe that Mr. Hollonbrook had committed suicide. And that left me with a puzzle that I knew I would not get out of my mind until I knew the answer.

My sleuthing that morning had gotten me absolutely nowhere except that I realized, as I should have realized in the beginning: A murder so cleverly committed had to be the result of careful planning. The best bet was that the planning had been done in Stedbury, North Carolina. But there was also a Borderville element, and that would have to be looked into right away before things could change too much.

You see, it was now exactly one week since Charles Hollonbrook had checked into the motel. And it was beans to doughnuts that the same personnel would be on duty that night at the Inn as had been on duty the week before. I needed to pay a little more attention to the Borderville end of my problem before I could hunt for an explanation at the North Carolina end.

So I went home and called Lona Champion and asked her to be my guest that evening for dinner at the Inn. She simply wouldn't have it that I was to pay for her dinner. Well, if she felt like that, I wasn't going to stand in her way.

We ate in the dining room, and it's very different at night from the way it is in the morning. We got there about 7:30 and ordered a nice dinner. I had lamb chops, a nice chef's salad, English peas, and a baked potato, with peach melba for dessert. It cost $7.50. Toward the end of the meal, it was quite dark outside, and the young man came around and lit the candle in the little glass cup on the table. They had turned on the under-water lights in the pool, and we could look out over the pool and see the young people with the lights on their young bodies as they swam about. How I used to love to swim! Well, Lona and I just had a good time.

When we were ready to leave, I told Lona to stay in her seat while I went to pay my bill. I left my pocketbook with her and told her to bring it along but not to get up for at least ten minutes.

I went to the cash register in the dining room and said to the cashier, "I just can't find my pocketbook. I don't suppose any-one has turned it in?"

She didn't look too well pleased with the idea that I didn't have the money to pay her; and no, she didn't know anything about my pocketbook.

"Maybe I ought to ask at the desk out there," I said with a big smile, like I had just thought of it.

She said, "Well, all right," or something like that.

So I went to the desk in the lobby. There was this good-looking girl there. I would say she was eighteen or twenty. She had lovely auburn hair that must have had a natural wave to it. She was tall and had a good figure—and great big blue eyes—not green—but just a little bit on the green side—and those big, long lashes. She was using more makeup than a girl that pretty needs to put on, and the clothes were just a shade too dressy for the job she was doing. But then, I could remember when I was like that. I had a slim figure when I was her age. I had blond hair and a lot of it. Oh, I thought I was something, and the boys did, too. What a time I gave my mother! I always was a lady, but I did everything a lady can do and still get away with it.

Anyhow, I said, "Honey, I don't suppose that somebody could have turned in a red leather purse, could they?"

She knew right away that nobody had brought in a red purse.

"Oh," I said, looking so distressed you would have thought I didn't know what on earth to do. "Oh, are you sure?"

She was sure. And so was I, because Lona had it, and I could just see Lona out of the corner of my eye, paying her check at the cash register.

I said, "What *will* I do?" and one or two other things that weren't any more sensible than that, until Lona could come up to me with my purse. Then I put on a big show about how happy I was to find my purse and how silly I had been to think it was lost and what would people think of me? Well, I hoped they would think I was harmless. That was what I was getting at with the whole show I was putting on.

So I walked over to the cashier and paid my bill, and the woman there looked happier. I walked back to the table and left a tip. Then I came back again to the desk in the lobby.

"Darling," I said to the young woman, "you were so sweet to me when I thought I had lost my purse. What is your name?"

"Teddy."

When I was young, teddies were women's underwear. But nothing is the same now.

"How unusual!" I said. "Is it short for Edwina?"

"Theodora," she said.

"What a lovely name, Theodora!" I said. "And what's the other name?"

"Brazille."

"Theodora Brazille—you ought to go on the stage or get into movies with that name and your good looks. Why, I think it is just lovely."

Praise is one thing people have no judgment about. They just never get enough of it. In that respect, Miss Brazille was no different from the general run of folks. And what I said was near enough to the truth that she didn't suspect a thing.

I tried the same thing I had tried on the little cleaning woman. "Have you worked here long?"

"Almost a year now," she said. I could tell she liked my compliment.

"Do you like the work?"

"Oh, it's all right."

"Well, working at this motel, you surely wouldn't want for excitement. Were you here at the desk when that man who killed himself checked in?" A look came into her eyes that said this was an uncomfortable topic.

"Oh," I said, "I suppose they don't want you to talk about it. But it was written up in the paper. There was such a long piece about it—when was it? Friday? But I didn't see your name there." Then I just looked at her and waited for her to say something.

"Oh, I checked him in, all right," she said after an awkward pause. The child could not avoid an answer, don't you see.

"I know the poor man must have seemed anxious and blue, with his mind made up to kill himself that way. I suppose you would notice."

"I didn't notice anything." She was just as nervous as a cat.

"Don't let it bother you," I said. "You're a darling child." I reached over and patted her hand.

I tried, but I couldn't get her to tell me whether there was anything unusual about Hollonbrook when he checked in—like agitation or melancholy. Her mind seemed to be occupied merely with the fact that one of the guests had taken his own life.

There is a reaction that young people have to death that is hard to remember when most of the folks you have known have long since passed on.

Nevertheless, I had done all that I could do at that point. I had talked to Fred Middleton, who saw the body before the police did. I had talked to the maid who had cleaned up the room, I had actually been in the room, and I had talked with the young woman who had checked Hollonbrook into his room some six or so hours before his death. That was pretty much all that I could do in Borderville. And it had gotten me nowhere.

I drove Lona home and then went home myself.

MY BRIEF CAREER AS A DETECTIVE

>> Henry Delaporte <<

It was a Tuesday morning. I had been at the office about an hour when Cindi, who handles our calls, informed me that Mrs. L. Q. C. Lamar Bushrow wished to talk to me.

"At least," she said, "that is what it sounded like."

And to be sure, there is only one Harriet Bushrow. "Put her through, Cindi," I said. "By all means, put her through."

"Mrs. Bushrow!" I exclaimed as soon as the connection was made. "So pleasant to hear from you! How can I help you?" This is my normal invitation to a caller, since helping people with problems is the way I make my living.

"Oh, Mr. Delaporte," she replied, "you are so kind to offer. As a matter of fact, I was trying to get your darling wife on the phone this morning; and when I couldn't get her, I called Lizzie Wheeler. Lizzie tells me that Helen didn't play for church yesterday. I hope there is nothing wrong."

I explained that our daughter, who was married last year, had just presented us with our first grandchild and Helen was in Indiana for a week on the pretext that only she knew how to take care of a baby just home from the hospital.

"How lovely!" Harriet cooed. The old girls with finishing-school educations know how to put just the right intonation on such expressions. And I admit that it sounded good to this first-time grandpa.

"Now, Mr. Delaporte," Harriet went on, "I have something I was going to ask of Helen, but since you are in such a good mood about that grandchild—is it a boy?"

"Yes," I said. "Weight: nine pounds."

"Oh, good gracious! And named Henry, I hope."

As a matter of fact, the tyke is Henry Delaporte Walters, though I pity the lad who has to confess such a name to his pals when he arrives at ten or twelve years.

"Oh, that's a lovely name. But I do want to ask you something." She cleared her throat with a ladylike cough. "I think you and Helen pretty generally go to Wilboro Beach each summer."

I pleaded guilty, and Harriet went on.

"Have you taken your vacation yet this year?"

I denied the accusation.

"But then, I suppose you will be going to Indiana to see that young man."

I explained that I had already been to Indiana and had come back by air, leaving Helen there to start her grandmotherly career. Helen was coming home on Friday, which would make it possible for her to play her services at the Episcopal church on Sunday, a duty that punctuates our lives with iron regularity.

There was a pause before Harriet went on. I know now that she had her campaign thoroughly planned and knew exactly what to do. She began in a slightly tentative tone. "Mr. Delaporte," she said, "I find conversations on the phone so impersonal and unsatisfactory, don't you?"

Now what is the answer to a question of that sort? I find no difficulty whatever in carrying on business by telephone. I mumbled something that sounded like "Well, now I don't know."

"Oh, I'm sure you must find it as difficult as I do. We could come to such a wonderful agreement if I could just see you for half a minute. Now I know you are just as busy as you can be, but do you think I could make an appointment with you at your office?"

And of course I could, and of course she came—that afternoon at 1:30.

Harriet is the widow of Lucius Quintus Cincinnatus Lamar Bushrow. The first four of those names belonged to a noted senator and U.S. Supreme Court justice from a distinguished Georgia family, and I understand that Mr. Bushrow was some sort of relative, which explains his long list of baptismal names. And the prominence of Justice Lamar explains why Harriet Bushrow insists upon using all the initials.

Harriet is close to ninety years old, though the average person would not suppose so from looking at her. Her energy is amazing, and she has the style that preempts the attention of all beholders.

I would guess that she is five feet seven, and she may weigh in at 175 or 170. But she is not dumpy. On the contrary, she holds her head high, and I imagine she was quite a beauty when she was young. As of now, she is handsome.

I don't know anything about fabrics, but when she came into my office she was garbed in some silky material—white with polka dots as big as quarters. She had on red shoes, carried a red pocketbook, and wore a large white straw hat with a circle of what appeared to be huge red poppies around the crown. I don't know much about styles; but since I have seen Harriet in the same outfit before, I know that the dress has seen several years of wear.

Still, with her favorite cut-crystal beads about her neck and her aristocratic features, she could have called herself a duchess and nobody would have dared deny it.

I bowed her into the client's chair.

"Now tell me what it is," I said.

"It's about that Mr. Hollonbrook," Harriet said.

"I see," I replied somewhat noncommittally.

"Oh, he was murdered, Mr. Delaporte. It wasn't suicide at all."

"The police think differently," I observed, "but I have a feeling you will try to convince me to the contrary." I had developed such admiration for this lady's powers of deduction during her investigation of the DAR Murder Mystery that I strongly suspected she was right. It was merely a matter of how she had reached her conclusion.

"Well," she said as she opened her eyes quite wide, "it is perfectly obvious." She pointed out that it was atypical of district governors to commit suicide. I had to admit that past events supported her theory.

Then she brought up the matter of the book *Break In* by Dick Francis. I have read the book, and I had to admit that I would never have committed suicide without having finished it—that is, assuming that I had gotten well into it.

"Now that 'suicide' note," she said, "there's nothing to that at all. People who commit suicide either leave no note or else they try to justify themselves or leave instructions. And that note did none of that. Besides, why would the man bring his memo pad to Borderville to write his farewell to the world?"

It was beyond question a paltry note. If I ever commit suicide, I hope I shall be able to contrive a more impressive explanation. Mrs. B. had gained her point.

"And think," she continued, "what inconvenience it would cause for him to commit suicide here in Borderville. He would have that long drive from home for nothing, and then the body would have to be taken back to North Carolina by the undertaker. And what about his car? Somebody would have to drive his car back down there. Then think of the inconvenience and embarrassment to the Borderville Rotary Club. Nobody with the responsibility of a district governor would put a club through that. There they would be with no speaker, and such a bust-up of everything!"

With this, too, I agreed.

"I believe Fred told me there was a silencer on the gun," she said. "Well, that's a how-do-you-do! So polite about not disturbing the other guests at the motel when he was putting everybody else to so much trouble. If he wanted to be private about it, why didn't he go off into the woods to blow his brains out?"

It had never occurred to me to blow my brains out, but I could see much in what she said.

"And did you ever see the man?"

I admitted I had not, and Harriet went on. "Well, neither have I, but I saw that picture they ran in the *Banner-Democrat*. And I know that picture was taken fifteen or twenty years ago. But if he still had any of that wavy hair, he wouldn't commit suicide in a way that would be detrimental to his good looks."

Harriet drew herself up as much as to say, Now you see which is the vain sex.

Then she pointed out that our district governor, before he retired for the night, had made preparations for the next day. "That," she said, "proves that he did not come here to commit suicide."

Again I granted her point.

After we had talked about it for some minutes, I said, "Yes, Mrs. Bushrow, all that you have gone over is true, and the whole thing is altogether unexplained. But even though we cannot reconcile the facts, there is still one element that can only be explained by the assumption that Charles Hollonbrook took his own life: The chain was on the door."

Mrs. B. gave me what was obviously meant to be her best smile. "I knew you would say that," she admitted. "And I don't know how to explain it. But he was killed in that room with the chain on the door, and so there must be some explanation." The smile lingered, daring me to find fault with her reasoning.

My wife is a northern girl, educated at Vassar. She does not stoop to womanly wiles; and in a way I am glad that she does not, for I would be forever at a disadvantage if she did. Still, it is a delight when the fair sex, even at advanced age, sees fit to use the full artillery.

Mrs. Bushrow did not wait for me to think up a rejoinder. Instead, she pressed her advantage: "We shall know how it was done when we know who did it. I am sure of that."

I believe that was putting the process hind-end-to. Nevertheless, there was a kind of logic there, which was to be proved by later events.

"And you have some idea who did it?" I said.

"Oh, it was someone who had cause," she replied. She seemed rather pleased with her answer, which, of course, was no more than a truism.

"Yes?" I said.

"Somebody wanted to kill him," Mrs. Bushrow announced, as though I could never have thought of such a thing.

When I didn't say anything, she went on. "I note once in a while that somebody is killed by a poor, deranged person who didn't even know the victim. But I don't imagine that happens very often. No, it is going to be somebody that knew Mr. Hollonbrook well—someone very close to him. People murder someone because they can't go on living with that person so close to them, perhaps threatening them or their peace of mind every day in the same house or office—or perhaps interfering with something important to that person—maybe fooling around with his wife or something like that. And that means that the man that kills and the man that gets killed are close in some way and the killer has to murder to get out of whatever it is that is compelling him."

"Then you are thinking of some one person specifically," I said.

"Why, of course," she said. "There is one person who is bound to inherit and would have access to the gun. I would hate to think that the poor man's wife did it. But then, that is the first thing that we must think. Mr. Delaporte, there are many reasons why a wife might wish to kill her husband. Perhaps he is cruel to her; perhaps he runs with other women; perhaps she is silly enough to think she loves another man. Then there are all sorts of little frictions; and if a woman doesn't have enough to occupy her mind, she can magnify these little frets until she is practically beside herself. Not that any of that is likely to be the case with Mrs. Hollonbrook, but we have to consider those things.

"Of course she would know where her husband would be staying and all that. Oh, I think the man's wife would be the first person we could think of.

"And then she is the only suspect that we know about right off. She is the logical point at which to start. And we know where she *says* she was when her husband was killed."

"And that was Wilboro Beach," I said, and grinned.

"You guessed it." Harriet returned my grin with a wink. "But we don't know that for a fact. The sheriff had such a hard time finding her. Now I just wish I knew exactly where she was staying in Wilboro Beach all that time."

"Very well," I said, "I can get the details from the sheriff's office and let you know. I'll be very glad to do it."

That was the wrong thing to say, because she came back immediately with "And then when you are in Wilboro, you will just check up on the alibi, won't you?"

It was not a request; it was a command. She had been right: A telephone conversation would not have served her purpose.

So there I was with Mrs. Bushrow's commission to verify the whereabouts of Mrs. Charles Hollonbrook on the night of May 26/27.

In fact, Helen and I had not planned to go down to Wilboro at all soon, but Mrs. B. had excited and directed my curiosity into a certain channel. As soon as Helen came home, I cleared my schedule, which fortunately I was able to do, and we went off to Wilboro.

Arriving at the beach, we enjoyed a shore dinner and went to our room that first night, glad that we were too old to think that we must dance or go to a movie or any of the other things that are obligatory for the young.

The next day bright and early, I looked at the address of Mrs. Hutton's Resort Accommodations, which had been given to me by the Ambrose County Sheriff's Office, and inquired at our motel how I might get there.

"Oh, yes," the room clerk said, "Mrs. Hutton was well known. She has been dead now for ten or fifteen years, but the place is run by her niece, a Mrs. Saunders." He said she had remodeled the place and that it was now very tony, very pricey, but he lamented that she did not pay her help "worth a damn."

He gave me directions, and I had no trouble finding the place.

Mrs. Hutton's was a two-story frame building with Victorian galleries across the entire front. Green rocking chairs adorned both the upper and the lower level. Although it was only 9:30 when I approached this structure, almost half of these rockers were already occupied.

I went in through the big double doors—open, of course, to catch the breeze coming off the ocean. The interior was very posh, with antique furniture and real oil paintings. At the desk, I asked for Mrs. Saunders and was told to wait.

Within a few minutes, Mrs. Saunders, a woman in perhaps her early sixties, appeared. She was smartly dressed, carefully coiffured, and obviously capable.

"Can I be of service, Mr. . . ." She consulted the card I had given to the desk attendant. "Mr. Delaporte?"

I explained my mission.

There was a slight pause. "Oh, yes," Mrs. Saunders said rather brusquely, "I am not likely to forget. What was it that you wanted to know?"

"Well," I said, "I would like to know exactly when she came and when she left."

"She came on May 25 and left about four-thirty on May 29."

"And was she here every day during that period?"

"As a matter of fact, she was not. When we got inquiries from the police and the undertaker and even the Rotary Club, I believe, we discovered that Mrs. Hollonbrook spent the night of the twenty-fifth with us; but on the twenty-sixth, twenty-seventh, and twenty-eighth, although she retained her room, the maid says the lady did not sleep here."

I don't know what answer to my question I had expected, but I certainly had not expected the answer that I received.

"You have no idea where she was during that time?"

"None whatever."

I had one other question. "When you finally contacted Mrs. Hollonbrook, what was her reaction?"

"Surprised—certainly. I think *surprised* is the best word."

"May I take it, then, that her reaction was less than what you would have expected of a wife who had just been informed of her husband's suicide?"

"Something of the sort."

"And did you tell the Ambrose County sheriff that?"

"The question did not come up."

Mrs. Saunders's information had been given from personal knowledge and with absolute assurance. There seemed, therefore, to be nothing further to ask. I thanked Mrs. Saunders and returned to my motel.

I confess that up to this point I had cooperated with Harriet Bushrow because she is a friend of my wife and I admire her spirit and intelligence and, quite frankly, because I was curious. But now it occurred to me that there was a very firm basis for suspicion in this case. District governors of Rotary frequently bring their wives with them, and the local Rotary Anns are required to entertain the distaff side of our governance.

It would not be a breach of decorum if the governor's wife did not accompany him. A district governor's wife may work or have home obligations, or she may merely be disinclined to go with the old boy. But even in this day of women's lib, one would scarcely expect a wife to hightail it to a beach resort the minute her husband leaves the house, rent a room at a high-priced place, and then go off mysteriously for three nights while the expense of the room continued. On the credit company's bill, it would look as though she had stayed in thoroughly proper accommodations during the whole period. How better and more safely might a woman play tag with her marriage?

I did not see how Hollonbrook's death in a locked room could be anything but suicide, but Harriet had assured me that if she found the murderer, she would be able to find how it was done. She had been brilliantly successful once before. Perhaps she could do the same in the Rotary Club Mystery, although I sincerely hoped that our little affair would never achieve such notoriety as to be the *Famous* Rotary Club Mystery.

AT THE READY

>> *Maud Tinker Bradfield* <<

Harriet Gardner and I were chums and roommates at Catawba
Hall—oh, so many years ago! Never did I have such a friend,
and never did we have such times as then—when women were
denied all forms of equality and freedom. But the beauty of it
was that we were young and having so much fun that we didn't
think much about other things.

In those days at a girls' school, there were no men around
except on designated occasions. And we thought those occasions were unduly rare. We weren't told about it, but one of the
reasons why our parents sent us to schools for girls only, was
that they *wanted* us to marry and they hoped that the instruction we received at such schools would help us do it. So we
were taught things that would make us the right kind of com-
panions for men of the sort that our parents hoped we would
find and marry.

What fun it was when the men *did* come to us! The Nuthaw
Military Institute was only seventeen miles away from us, and a
train from Nuthaw arrived in Catawba in the evenings at 7:09
and a train from Catawba arrived in Nuthaw at 10:15. That did
not leave much time for us to see our beaux on "permitted"

evenings, but oh, what good use we did make of those three hours!

Jay was a cadet at Nuthaw, as was Lamar Bushrow, and those boys managed to see us, permitted or not, at least once every week. I won't talk about Jay except to say that he was mine and quite satisfactory; but since Harriet is the subject of my tale, I will say something about Lamar.

He was just about the handsomest thing anyone ever saw. He stood six feet tall and was slim in the hips and broad in the shoulders. He had beautiful blond wavy hair and a tiny mustache. All the girls swooned over him. But he had eyes only for Harriet.

Now don't get the notion that Jay and Lamar were our only beaux. That would be entirely wrong. Harriet was quite a popular girl. There were always three or four cadets who called on her at the same time. I had several beaux, too, but never as many as Harriet had.

Actually, I feel sorry for girls now, who usually seem to have just one beau. When we were besieged with two or three at a time, we had no opportunity to get serious (until the right time came along) or to get into trouble. But did we mind? Not at all. To sit on a veranda on a May evening with three or four young men trying their best to please while each attempted to outdo the others is very pleasant to a young woman.

So it all came back to me when I got Harriet's letter—dear Harriet, who was always so much fun! She was taller than I and looked like a princess, and there was no mischief she and I did not get into. How well she played the part of Tony Lumpkin in the class play! I was Miss Neville, but Harriet got all the applause. And I admit that she deserved all of it.

But back to Harriet's letter.

It was so good to hear from Harriet; we had always corresponded at the necessary times—such as birthdays, special occasions, and, of course, whenever one of the old girls of dear old Catawba passed on. But I was really surprised when Harriet proposed a visit, and even more surprised and thrilled when she explained her reason for coming.

Harriet had written to me about the DAR business, and I had read all about it in the papers and in *Time* magazine, and then, too, she had sent me the book when it came out. But now she was on another detective case and she was asking *me* to help her!

Don't think that I have been exactly comatose all my life. Jay and I had three children, a son who lives in California, another in Kentucky, and a daughter who lives here in Stedbury. We all had a very happy life. Jay did very well in insurance, and we got to do a lot of things that were interesting. We went to Europe three times. And we had enough money that I could collect old silver in a modest way. And then, too, I had my painting, and it was lots of fun when one of my pictures took a ribbon in a competition. But I am too shaky now to paint anything but daubs. Since Jay has been gone, it didn't make sense to hang on to all of that silver, and I sold it. I got rid of our big house, and now I have this little place that is just right for me.

So my life has been less exciting during the last few years. I had just decided that the only career left me was that of "old lady."

Now Harriet was opening a vista of intrigue and excitement, and I could hardly wait.

The appointed day and the estimated hour came, and, sure enough, pretty soon I heard a car draw up in front of the house. Someone got out, and I heard "Yoo-hoo!"

I tell you it took years off my age. I ran to the door, and there was Harriet coming up the walk—no longer so tall and by no means so slim—but Harriet nevertheless, still with the spring in her personality, if no longer in her step.

Lord, how we hugged and kissed! It knocked her hat catawampus.

I showed her my guest room. We brought her things in, and I gave her a few minutes to use the powder room. Then we sat down together in the living room.

"It was such a thrill to get your letter!" I said. "And I have been thinking every day about what you wrote in it."

"I'll tell you," Harriet said, dabbing at her forehead with a little lace handkerchief—the air conditioning in her car had gone bad on her. "I wouldn't have taken on this little matter if I hadn't thought, Well now, Stedbury, North Carolina! Won't I have fun down there with Maud, and won't we work on this together. You *have* been sniffing around, haven't you? And you *can* tell me all about this Hollonbrook?"

Of course I knew something about Charles Hollonbrook and his marriages and shenanigans of various kinds. Stedbury used to be so small, hardly anybody knew where it was, and so we mostly knew what everybody in town was doing. But then the Second World War came along, and we really grew because we had our own war plant. When the war was over, our prosperity kept up for quite a while. We are much larger today than we used to be. So, while I knew something about the Hollonbrooks, it is harder to keep up with what goes on now, and I am out of so many things in which I used to be quite active.

I knew, of course, that "Holly" Hollonbrook—that's what they call him—came here right from Vietnam. We all thought he and his wife were such a sweet couple. And then there was the Hollonbrook divorce and another marriage—to his secretary, a very pretty young woman, whom I have seen many times at the club. And, of course, Holly came into Rotary, and Jay knew him in that way.

I know more about Linda, the first wife, than I do about Alice, because Linda and I use the same beauty shop. Nothing ever goes right for poor Linda. Whether or not she is justified, I cannot say, but she constantly complained that Holly did not give her enough money.

There was, I believe, an original agreement, but as Holly

became more and more successful, Linda was always insisting that he owed her and the children more and more. It had been arranged that the children were to spend so much time with their mother and so much time with their father. But before long, they spent almost all their time with Linda.

The children did not like Alice. I dare say Linda had something to do with that. There were all kinds of problems, and I don't remember the details. But there was a time there when I couldn't go to the beauty parlor without hearing the whole thing, beginning to end, two or three times.

The upshot was that Holly agreed to increase the support if Linda would take sole responsibility for the children. Holly got it in writing, and, according to Linda, he never raised it above the agreed amount from that time on.

It was only to be expected that the children's expenses would increase as they got older and went into high school; and with college coming on, Linda probably has grounds for complaint.

I understand that Linda's people had a little money. But her father became an invalid, and I get the impression that there is very little left there. So Linda started a dress shop and carried it on for a few years. Then she tried a health-food store. It did very well as long as the health-food fad was strong, but I guess people are getting a little tired of that now, because she closed her shop about a year ago.

Now, Linda is fairly active in the Methodist church. I have friends who think that she is very much put-upon. But I can see why she might not be just the wife that Charles J. Hollonbrook wanted.

After Holly and Alice were married, they joined the Episcopal church, and they seem to fit in over there. (I am just a good old Baptist.)

I told Harriet all about this. When I had finished, she said, "Now let's look at the people who don't like him. I have written down his first wife. I guess she goes by Linda Hollonbrook." Harriet had her little memorandum book out, and a pencil.

"And you say the poor woman is bitter?"

I have always tried to see the best side of Linda. I don't approve of men who shed their wives and children just because their family no longer pleases them. But I must admit that I had painted Linda Hollonbrook as a bitter woman.

"Surely you don't think Linda could have killed Holly!" I said.

Harriet tilted her head back and gave me that look I know so well. "That depends," she said. "Now tell me some more. Did he have a secretary?"

"Well, yes."

"What about her?"

"Just a secretary, I would say. Do you think Holly may have been playing around with her the same way he did with Alice?"

"You know what the Bible says," Harriet replied. " 'The dog shall return to his vomit and the old hog to his wallowing in the mire.' "

Well, I couldn't visualize Charles J. Hollonbrook with his pretenses having an affair with Paula Stout. You see, I know her. She is a sweet little mouse of a person and a pillar of the Baptist church.

So I said, "Just wait until you see her, and make up your own mind about her."

"Good enough," said Harriet, and she wrote down Paula's name. Then she said, "Now tell me about his business." Of course I remembered when he and his partner, Vic Douglass, came to town. But they broke up.

I really couldn't remember just how that went. I knew that after the split, Victor Douglass didn't do very well, and Arlene, Vic's wife, sniffs whenever Holly's name is mentioned.

Harriet looked at her notes and underlined one or two things. "Is there anything else that you can think of?" she asked.

There wasn't. I had told her everything I could think of just at that moment—though it did seem that I ought to know more.

We sat there for a while, both of us trying to think what else there might be.

"What's the name of your paper here in Stedbury?" Harriet asked.

It is the *Gazette*.

Harriet said, "I think I'll go to your public library tomorrow and see what I can find in their files."

It was a good idea. You see, Charles Hollonbrook was so much younger than Jay and I that he and his wives didn't mean anything to us except for Rotary. And now that Jay is gone, I don't really keep up with Rotary the way I used to. So all I know about the Hollonbrooks is just whatever gossip drifts somehow into my world, which has become smaller—oh so much smaller without Jay.

>> *Harriet Bushrow* <<

When we were working on the DAR Mystery, Helen Delaporte and Margaret and Lizzie and I had the advantage that we were in our own hometown. There were four of us. So what one didn't know or find out, another did. And we just shared our information the same way people share food at a covered-dish luncheon, and it came out fine. I happened to be the one who was fortunate enough to be there when the last piece of information fell into place—that's all.

But Stedbury, North Carolina, is not my hometown. And no matter how helpful Maud was, I would still be at a disadvantage because I knew nothing about the place.

I tell you, small towns are about the best entertainment a woman with good sense can have. There is nothing at the movies—murder, spies, romance, scandal, heartbreak, comedy, horror—even happy endings sometimes—nothing at the movies that isn't right there in that town keeping people entertained around the calendar. And it is all very instructive, too.

But all the things that happen in a small town pass, and one person will remember this thing, while another will remember that. Still, if the local paper is any good, all the public facts will be there—just the bare bones, of course. But that would give me something to ask about.

Maud had said that Charles Hollonbrook came to Stedbury after he got home from the Vietnam War. Well, to an eighty-eight-year-old woman, that's not so long ago. And I figured that this little local *Gazette* was not going to be a big thick thing. So it shouldn't have been too much of a task to run through those back issues—just a few days. I would be interested only in items about Hollonbrook. And I imagined that after a while I would get a good-enough picture of the things related to him, and it wouldn't take any time at all.

That was what I thought then. How little I knew!

The Carnegie Library is on a tree-lined street—not a big building at all—just typical of the libraries Mr. Carnegie used to finance. It looks about like the one he built in 1912 in Gloriosa, Georgia, where I grew up.

Behind the library is a nice shady parking lot, where you can park your car all day and it won't be hot when you come back.

Of course there were steps going up to the front door—who ever heard of a Carnegie Library without steps?—and the two iron lampposts to either side and the huge frosted globes.

The inside of the library was also like the one in Gloriosa—golden oak. We used to think that golden oak was the only thing to have. They tell me that sort of thing is coming back through restoration and all that. Well, Stedbury won't have to restore its library, because it is all there—even to the plaster statue of Athena on a pedestal.

There was that old-time library smell, too—furniture polish, floor wax, old books, and just a whiff of disinfectant from the rest rooms. It felt like something I'd always known.

But some things change. When I went up to the librarian's desk, there behind it on a table was a computer and the librarian, with her back to me, clicking away on one of those little keyboards.

The sign on the desk read, MS. LAURA FOLSOM, LIBRARIAN. So I supposed that Ms. Laura must be as modern as her computer.

I coughed just a little and said, "Beg pardon."

Miss Folsom turned her swivel chair around. She looked to be in her late forties, and I pledge you my word she had a yellow pencil behind her ear—a pencil with one of those big erasers stuck on the end of it. I said to myself, Good Lord, she's an old maid in spite of everything! You know they don't make them like that anymore.

But she was just as nice as she could be and said something about what could she do for me and so on.

I explained that I wanted to see the files of the Stedbury *Gazette.*

Well, they were stored upstairs, all except the last three years. Those were at the *Gazette* office and would be until the *Gazette* saw fit to transfer them to the library. She pressed the button on her desk. In half a minute, a nice young man—still had pimples on his face—came up, and I told him the dates I wanted. Then he went off to get those big old books.

Miss Folsom said, "I don't believe you are one of our regular patrons."

"Oh no," I said. "I'm a visitor here in town."

"Then you must sign our guest book," she said.

I don't know what anyone ever does with a guest book, but everywhere you go you seem to find one. And, of course, I was waiting for my books to come downstairs. So I signed—it was no more than polite to do so.

Well, I tell you! I had no idea what I was asking that poor boy to do when I sent him to get those newspapers. Eighteen great huge volumes. It just seemed that he kept going back again and again to get more of them.

Miss Folsom said, "I believe it would be best if I wiped those things off first." You never saw such a cloud of dust as rose from those old papers. I apologized for the inconvenience.

"I think," she added, "that since these volumes are so big and heavy, we'll just let you look at them in the workroom."

Well that was fine, because I saw right away that I would be taking more than just a day or two to go through all that big pile, and Miss Folsom said I could leave everything there until I had finished.

So I got out my pencil and memorandum book and got right to work.

In the issue of August 21, 1969, I first found the ad in the real estate section: Hollonbrook and Douglass. So that was the beginning of my search.

Then in every issue of the paper there was just ad after ad after ad—Hollonbrook and Douglass. Those young men must have been very aggressive. And I noticed from the properties listed in their ads that whatever they advertised, they soon sold. Of course, some of their deals probably were not so good, but in comparison with other realtors in Stedbury, they were doing mighty well.

Then in September, about a year after Hollonbrook came to town, there was a story about him on the sports page, where I almost missed it. What it said was: "Local Man Proves Himself in Rifle Meet." The local man was Charles (Holly) Hollonbrook. The story called him a "popular young newcomer to Stedbury and decorated war veteran" and told how he had come back from the Western North Carolina Target Shooting Association's competition with the Bernard S. Thorpe trophy, winning over eighteen contestants.

The next item I found was the birth announcement of a son, James Andrew, to Mr. and Mrs. Charles J. Hollonbrook.

That would make the boy old enough to be a suspect. I hated to think the son would murder his father. But we read about that sort of thing all the time, and Maud had said the father kept the boy short on money.

So I made a note about young James—to look into later, you understand.

The next September, there was another trophy from the rifle competition. I would say shooting a rifle at a target is an appropriate recreation for a man with the drive and competitive spirit I was beginning to admire in Charles Hollonbrook. And all the time, there were ads, ads, ads. He was driving right along in his business—he was obviously the kind of man who just has to win.

Then in the spring of 1974, I came across this: HOLLONBROOK ORGANIZES HANDGUN CLUB. That's the headline. Then the story went on: "Charles (Holly) Hollonbrook, popular realtor and firearms enthusiast, invites all interested in handgun marksmanship to join the recently organized Stedbury Handgun Club." There was more, giving date and place of meeting and all that, and it was stated that "an immediate effort" would be made "to secure an arrangement with the Stedbury Police Force for the use of the municipal pistol range."

I used to shoot a pistol. Papa thought every young woman should know how to shoot, and he would take me out to the farm, where I would shoot tin cans off the fence. I never was very good at it, but I felt very raffish and worldly shooting like that.

Well, to get back to that pistol-shooting club of Charles (Holly) Hollonbrook's, that was very interesting because Hollonbrook was killed with his own gun. And somebody in that club might be able to shed some light on how that could happen. So I made a note to investigate the club.

The next thing I found was a story about a new industrial plant that was coming to Stedbury. Charles (Holly) Hollonbrook—in those days, the *Gazette* always put the parentheses in the middle of the name—was quoted as knowing all about it. And two days later, there was an editorial congratulating Charles (Holly) Hollonbrook for bringing Featherstone Plastics to Stedbury. The *Gazette* seemed to think that Charles (Holly) Hollonbrook had done it almost alone.

You would think that after bringing a business like Featherstone to town, Holly and his partner would be as happy as pigs in the mud. But just a month later, I noticed from the ads that Hollonbrook and Douglass weren't partners anymore. And there, don't you see, was something I needed to look into.

Now you folks reading this are probably going to say that I was just letting my imagination run on and on, as I found something suspicious in nearly everything I picked up about Charles Hollonbrook in the *Gazette*. But the imagination is where important things happen. Columbus imagined that the world was round. And Edison imagined that an electric light would work. And what about men on the moon? Remember when that only happened in the funny papers? Well, all of that starts in the imagination.

Imagination is like dough rising. It just works and works until it rises to a proper condition. Then the cook punches it down and lets it work again until it is right for the oven.

I kept on looking and found the birth announcements of the two Hollonbrook girls. I suppose a feminist would insist that they were just as likely to murder their dad as a boy would be, but I didn't think so.

The next thing I found was the divorce. That was in the legal notices. Hard times can cause divorce, and too much success can cause divorce. I could only speculate, but in this case I was laying the blame on success.

I just read till my eyes were tired, and then it was 4:45. I had worked right straight through since nine o'clock except for lunch at a little restaurant with Maud. And now the library was about to close. Miss Folsom came up to the table where I was working. She had a book in her hand. It was *The Famous DAR Murder Mystery*.

"You are Harriet Bushrow," she said.

I had to admit it.

"It is such an honor to have you use our library!"

It flashed all over me that I had made a bad mistake when I had written my name in that guest book. I might have known that a librarian would recognize it. And then it wouldn't take her ten minutes to figure out why I was reading all those old Stedbury *Gazettes*. And soon it would be all over town.

"Would you please autograph my personal copy of *The Famous DAR Murder Mystery?*" she said, "I would be so grateful."

So that was that.

I spent another day in the library and found that Holly had been in the Junior Chamber and had participated in their follies as a chorus girl! And then he got married again, to Miss Alice Ritchie—married in the Methodist church. Of course, that would be the same church the first wife belonged to. It had been almost two years since the divorce and was the first marriage of the second wife, so nobody could criticize *her*. But I bet a lot was said about *him*.

There were other developments: He showed up on the committee for the annual charity drive, and the next year he was the chairman of that committee. A little later, Mr. and Mrs. Charles Hollonbrook (without the parentheses from here on) were on the committee for the New Year's dance at the country club. A few months later, Mr. Charles J. Hollonbrook was elected to the vestry at St. Barnabas Episcopal Church. And he was on the board of the Salvation Army. Surprising? Not at all. It was just what I would have expected.

Of course, the files lacked three years of coming up to the present. During that time, Holly would have been president of the Stedbury Rotary Club and just this year district governor.

I found that I had made quite a few notes of things I ought to think about. I had just about decided that Stedbury wasn't very different from Borderville. Matter of fact, probably not all that different from the town where you live.

Back at Maud's house that evening, as I looked over my notes, I found that I hadn't turned up any surprising facts, but I had formed a definite picture in my mind of Charles Hollonbrook's personality.

Whatever else he was, it was forceful the way he came into

this little town and started up from nothing. Little towns don't always welcome that kind of thing. Most times, little towns think they exist for the benefit of the people who are already there. There will be one big, important family, along with another that is not quite so big or important. These two families won't like each other, but they will agree that outsiders should stay away unless the outsider has formed an alliance with one of the families through marriage. Inlaws have to be accommodated, but even in the case of inlaws it takes a long time to be naturalized.

Yet Charles Hollonbrook breezed into town with another newcomer and began to sell real estate right and left. Just think of it. He got himself into the country club and on the vestry at the Episcopal church, not to mention that he got to be president of the local Rotary Club and finally Rotary district governor. It seemed to me that he had just about made himself into an insider. But at the same time, that feat cannot be accomplished, no matter how cleverly and diplomatically it is done, without making enemies. Not all of the enemies would murder—I hope, but there must be some, at least, who would not be sorry he was dead.

Well, we have to admire Charles Hollonbrook for his success in what you would call a hostile environment. But there is always that downside to the record, too. You see, he broke up his partnership in just a few years and then very soon his marriage. Whose fault was it? If it was just the one bust-up, I might give the young man the benefit of the doubt. But two things like that?

I was to learn quite a bit more about Charles (Holly) Hollonbrook, as well as Charles J. Hollonbrook.

IN WHICH I RECEIVE MORE THAN A MASSAGE

>> Harriet Bushrow <<

You'll never guess what I've done for you," Maud said when I got back to the house.

Of course I had no idea.

"I've made an appointment for you with a masseuse."

What on earth could the woman have been thinking of? I'd never had a massage in my life, and I had no idea of such a thing now.

"Now, Hattie, don't look at me like that. The notion just struck me this morning, and I went right to the phone and made the appointment—ten-thirty tomorrow morning." Maud laughed, then she began to explain.

They have a very lovely country club at Stedbury, and several years ago the town banker insisted that they install a steam room and hire a masseur. Of course, that's for men and operates only in the afternoons. But in the mornings, the masseur's wife gives massage to the ladies, although the steam bath doesn't go with it. The woman's name is Noralou Passmore. Maud says the girl is well named: She knows more and she passes it on.

"Get her started on the subject of Charles Hollonbrook, and you'll hear enough to make your ears ache."

And that's how I came to have a massage from Noralou.

The Stedbury Country Club couldn't have been in a more beautiful location. The town is in the Piedmont, and that means that on beautiful clear days, if you are in the right place, you see the Blue Ridge Mountains, hazy and soft to the northwest.

Well the clubhouse is in exactly the right place for that view. It is lovely.

When I first walked into the club, I didn't see a soul. Off to the left, I peeked through a door at the ballroom. It is handsome and freshly done up by a decorator—not my taste—but expensive and impressive.

To the right of the ballroom was the dining room, with a carpet almost as thick as and about the color of the greens outside. I was wondering how I could find out where to go when a young woman with a stack of tablecloths in her arms came through a swinging door. She told me how to go downstairs and follow the hall to the right and then to the left. And when I did all that, sure enough I was in the right place; and there was Noralou. I introduced myself. "I know," she said. "You're the lady from Tennessee that is staying at Miz Bradfield's."

"I've never had a massage before," I said, "and I didn't know what kind of clothes I ought to put on."

"Well, honey," she said, "for a massage we just take them all off."

I judge she meant *I* took them all off, for she had on one of those warm-up suits—it very likely had been magenta, but it looked to have been through the wash a good number of times. It made her resemble a pink Mack truck.

"What must I do?" I asked.

"There's a dressin' room right there," she said. "Just take off your clothes and wrap this sheet around you, and come back here."

Well, I did; and when I came out, I know I looked like one of the women at the tomb of Jesus in a Sunday-school pageant.

"Now get up on this table and lie on your tummy."

I have to acknowledge that my "tummy" is not the smallest thing I can lie on. I was glad there was nobody but Noralou to see me trying to get in that position and retain my modesty with that sheet wrapped around me. And no sooner did I get settled than Noralou peeled the sheet back and began working me over, starting with my shoulders and neck.

"Just relax, honey," she crooned, "Noralou is going to do all the work."

"Oh, that feels good," I said. "Have you done this kind of work always?"

"I commenced when I was nineteen, and I'm thirty-nine now. Bill and me have been at the club ten of those years, and I reckon we'll stay on. The massage business don't have as good a reputation nowadays with all these 'massage parlors.' "

Noralou's voice rose in disgust.

"It's hard on those of us that's professional. Me and Bill are born-again Christian people and wouldn't do—you know—somethin' that wasn't professional. Massage is a 'healing art.' "

Again Noralou's voice rose, but in a tone somewhere in the neighborhood of holy awe. Well, I saw that she could probably go on about the massage business. While a discourse on massage parlors by a born-again Christian might be very interesting, that wasn't what I wanted to hear.

"With all that trashy, immoral massage parlor business," I said—and I made it sound right disgusting, which it is—"you are really fortunate to work in such a lovely club."

"Well, me and Bill do all right," Noralou observed with considerable satisfaction.

"I'd imagine you have a very high-class clientele here," I said.

"You hit it right, there," she agreed. "The club don't have but only very select members. Of course, some of them—but I won't say anything about that. Lots of rich people in this club, and me and Bill do all right."

"Maybe you knew that poor gentleman that committed suicide in Borderville last month."

"Mr. Hollonbrook." Noralou said it as if she had just adjusted her frame of reference and was ready to go.

"Yes," I said, "I believe that was his name."

"Mr. Holly Hollonbrook, poor soul. Killed hisself up there in Tennessee. Is that the town you come from?"

"Yes," I said.

"Well what do you know?" This, of course, was not a question, but a prelude.

"Why, I'll say I knew that poor soul—know Miz Hollonbrook a lot better—real nice lady—always gives a real good tip. But I can tell you, she had a lot to put up with about him—poor soul—taking his own life that way! But he's paying for it now." She kneaded away for a moment in silence.

"And such a fine-lookin' man!" she continued. "It seemed like he about had everything. But still everybody has their own private life. And the Good Book says we hadn't ought to judge."

"Are you saying he wasn't just what he ought to have been?" I suggested.

"Well," Noralou admitted, "now that you mention it, I have to say he sure wasn't. It's a terrible thing when somebody takes their own life, but let me tell you, there's folks in this town that thinks he done us a favor when he killed hisself."

"Why do you say that?" I asked. There was no need to urge Noralou, but I did so anyhow. Her pause was only artistic punctuation.

"Honey, it was women." Noralou made it sound like something out of the garbage can.

"Now I know what men are like," she continued, "and I guess I'm as forgiving as the next one. But there's a limit. Folks talk about him and his first wife and how he divorced her to marry the one that's now his widow.

"I don't have a thing against her, mind you. She's a member here and just as nice as you please. Always generous and nice. And the divorce and all that happened before me and Bill came to work here, but they say she was his secretary. Some say she caused the divorce, and some say it was the first wife's fault; and it was only natural with a pretty secretary that she would be the second misses.

"But that don't excuse him."

By this time, Noralou had peeled the sheet clear down below my hips and was working away at the small of my back. It just felt wonderful, but I was so interested in what the woman was saying that I didn't pay much attention to what she was doing.

"I guess you mean he had affairs," I said.

"Affairs! I couldn't begin to tell you."

But she *did* begin, and did a right good job of it, too.

"It was about five years ago," she said. "We had this new pro here at the club. Now pros are men just like any other men. And working at a golf club, you see pros make passes now and then. But Bucky Patterson had this cute little wife, Desiree, and he was just crazy about her. He spent every penny he had on her, and she was a doll.

"Bucky was good-looking, too—brown wavy hair and blue eyes and good buns. She had no call to turn her eyes to another man.

"But that Chuck Hollonbrook! Him with his Lincoln Continental and his Rolex watch. Not much of a golf player, but he'd swagger into the club with his golf bag like he was Arnold Palmer."

"Noralou," I said, "I don't think you liked him."

"Roll over," she ordered, giving a little pat to my behind. There hadn't been a pat like that in a long, long time.

"I'll tell you, Bucky Patterson was as nice a fellow as you

would ever want to meet. He just had stars in his eyes whenever that wife of his came around.

"So what happened was that Mr. Hollonbrook began sucking up to Bucky—the way some men do to professional athletes. It was 'Bucky' this and 'Bucky' that and 'Come on, have a drink on me.'

"Not that Bucky was the kind that was in the bar all the time, or Mr. Hollonbrook, either. But it started in the bar.

"First there would be just Bucky and Mr. Hollonbrook—for a cocktail before going home to dinner. Then it was Mr. and Mrs. Hollonbrook—Alice, her name is—and Bucky and Desiree—cocktails, of course—and then dinner here at the club, the four of them.

"I don't know when Mr. Hollonbrook and Desiree began shacking up, but I know when Bucky found out. Bucky had this friend who was going to the Augusta Open, and Bucky went down there with him. Well, the friend got sick and Bucky had to drive him home earlier than he had expected.

"When Bucky got to the house, the papers were laying on the front porch, and the mail hadn't been brought in for three days. No Desiree! Bucky started calling around—couldn't imagine what had happened. Thought maybe her mother had got sick—or maybe a death of some relative.

"And then. . . ."

Noralou would rate pretty high on my list of storytellers. *And then*—indeed! She wanted me to ask—to be her stooge, so as to throw the emphasis on the climax.

"Well, go on," I said. "Tell the rest."

"Mr. Hollonbrook drove up in front of the house and let Desiree out. That's what happened. And as she came tripping up the walk with her little overnight bag and her suitcase, who should open the front door but Bucky!

"I'd give a pretty to have been there.

"Poor Bucky! Miz Bushrow, he idolized that girl. And this day and age, when a man is like that, a woman hadn't ought to play around. No ma'am.

"What made it worse, you see, is that Mr. Hollonbrook was on the board of the club. And Jake Robinson, that was the club manager then, was one of these kind that knows where his bread is buttered. I mean him and Mr. Hollonbrook was like peas in a pod, they was so close.

"Poor Bucky! Next time he got a chance, him and Mr. Hollonbrook got into a fight down by the ninth hole. It must have been a regular knock-down-and-drag-out. Mr. Hollonbrook had a bruise on his cheek bigger'n a biscuit and downright purple. And poor Bucky got his lip cut something awful. Why, they had to take stitches.

"And that Jake Robinson—he was the meanest old thing anyway, and a few months later they caught him stealing money from the club, and that was the last of him—but anyhow, Jake Robinson, being hand in glove with Mr. Hollonbrook, he tried to fire Bucky on the spot.

"And Bucky said he was going to sue the club for breach of contract. And Jake said if he did, Mr. Hollonbrook would have Bucky up for assault and battery. And Bucky said if Mr. Hollonbrook did that, he would name Mr. Hollonbrook in his divorce suit, and there were a good many other things he could tell about Mr. Hollonbrook.

"Maybe you don't think that put the monkey on somebody else's back!

"Well, so Jake said the club would buy Bucky's contract, and Bucky said that wasn't good enough. Then Jake said he could get Bucky a job at a club in Florida. So that sounded pretty good, and Bucky took it."

"My goodness," I exclaimed. "Now the pro," I said. "What did you say his name was?"

"Bucky Patterson."

"Bucky," I mused. "Is that his real name?"

"Real name—Buchannan."

"Ah," I said. "And where did you say he went?"

"Playa Grande Club, near Lauderdale."

Now that's a good long distance from Borderville, and the whole story took place a long while ago. Nevertheless, Mr. Buchannan Patterson was an item of interest.

"And did Bucky and his wife get back together?" I asked.

"Lord, no! He got that divorce, and she and him both left town."

"And what about Mr. Hollonbrook?"

"He faced it out. You never saw such a thing in your life."

"Didn't folks talk about it?"

"Honey, you can bet your sweet life they did. But Mr. Hollonbrook with his money, and Miz Hollonbrook taking it cool as you please, it kind of passed over. And then some said that little Desiree was just a fool. And to tell the truth, she was. I don't know what become of her."

"Did Bucky marry again?"

"He might have, but I doubt it. You never saw anybody so broke up as he was."

Maud had certainly been right about Noralou. But whether or not it had gotten me anywhere, I was not certain.

Anyhow, I got myself dressed again and asked Noralou how much I owed her. And do you know, that sweet Maud had told her to add my massage to *her* bill there at the club. So I gave Noralou a five-dollar tip. I certainly wouldn't know, but I hoped that was a handsome tip. I wouldn't want Noralou talking about *me*.

Maud had arranged to meet me in the club dining room for lunch. She was already seated at the table when I got there. That girl was always pretty, but it just seems that age was good to her. She was a picture in a gray silk suit with a frilly white blouse and great big pink pearl ear bobs and necklace—fake, of course—I don't even know if real pearls are ever pink. But they ought to be, for they certainly were becoming to Maud.

Her sweet blue eyes were just flashing as I came to the table;

I could tell she had something really exciting to tell me. But she said we should order first.

I selected the chicken-salad croissant, and Maud ordered quiche. Then as soon as the girl had left with our orders, Maud said, "You'll not guess who wants to talk to you."

Well, I couldn't imagine. So I told Maud I would just give up.

"It's the widow," she said.

At first, I didn't get the idea, but Maud explained that Mrs. Alice Hollonbrook had called and wanted to talk to me.

I want you to know that was a surprise to me. I had been wondering how I could work it around so it would seem natural for me to talk to her and ask her a lot of questions—and most of all about her *alibi*—and here she had called me! But then I reflected that Ms. Folsom at the library had penetrated my disguise.

Well, if it had got me access to Alice Hollonbrook, perhaps it was not such a bad thing that Ms. Folsom had published my presence to Stedbury.

MY STORY

>> *Alice Hollonbrook* <<

Perhaps you are surprised to see that I have joined the staff and am contributing my bit to the story of how my husband's murder was disguised as suicide and how the murderer was found.

I warned Mrs. Bushrow that it was a bad idea to include me in the number of narrators. You see, it removes me from the list of suspects—but this is what she wanted, and this is what it is going to be.

In a way, it is appropriate that I should participate in the Rotary Mystery, because I am what was formerly called a Rotary Ann, the widow, in this case, of a Rotarian—one who was president of his club and governor of his district. And, I hasten to add, regardless of the peccadilloes and larger flaws of Holly's character, he was truly supportive of Rotary and was a good officer. Though his tremendous ambition was certainly served by the offices he held, I assure you that in his official activities he actually did put service above self.

I suppose Rotarians are only like the rest of us with all our faults. But there is something about Rotary that brings out the best in its members. Rotary calls for the same amount of loyalty to the local club as any other organization does: attendance—

oh how loyal Holly was to that—dues, committees. Rotary could justify itself merely at that level when you think of fifty-two meetings a year. And as a visitor, I have heard some of their programs; frankly, most weren't that good. Still, look at it this way: Those programs, good and bad, on topics of local importance, keep a cross section of community leaders informed about city government, schools, industrial developments, and many, many other things of real usefulness.

Rotary is above all a service organization. The Stedbury Rotary Club built the ball field for the Boys Club, gives five thousand a year to Theater Stedbury, provides loans at low interest to college students from our area, assists the Janie Boyer Home, the Shelter for Battered Women, and the Downtown Association, which is fighting civic decay—not to mention the annual Rotary Charity Fund and assistance to the Salvation Army.

That's just what Rotary does at the local level. And believe me, it doesn't stop there. Rotary is truly international. It has clubs all over the world and promotes exchange of ideas by sending and receiving teams of experts to and from everywhere. Last year, the Stedbury club was visited by a team from Venezuela—just delightful people, whom we got to know and like. Although they were here to study and did study, it would have been worth the effort if the visit produced nothing but friendship.

And don't forget the Paul Harris Foundation. Its funds are used for various things, but most recently they have been used to combat polio worldwide. In fact, polio has been virtually eliminated through the work of the Paul Harris Foundation.

I don't think that the organization's reputation should be tarnished merely because an individual Rotarian may not have been a paragon. Rotary simply represents what is best in the way we live today. And if there is something wrong, it is wrong not with Rotary but with us.

Well, what am I doing preaching? There is as much wrong with me as there is with any of us. Holly's death has brought me to think about a good many things I had figured would be put off for a long, long time.

As soon as I heard that *the* Harriet Bushrow was in town, it flashed through my mind that she was here because of Holly's death. I knew all about Harriet because her book, *The Famous DAR Murder Mystery,* was reviewed at my study club. We were studying the achievements of Appalachian women. Brenda Miller had chosen the book because she thought it said something about the region—and a lot about feminine initiative.

So Harriet Bushrow didn't think Chuck had committed suicide. And neither did I. But I had better get on with what happened during our visit.

When the door chimes sounded, I was not prepared for the commanding figure I was to find at my door. She looked like— well, she looked like the Queen Mother. Not that Harriet seems haughty—nobody could be more down-to-earth. It is something in the way she holds her head—and those clear gray eyes look at you with absolute assurance, as though she sees you through and through and is considering what she will do with you.

She had on the hat with the red poppies—and, of course, the famous cut-crystal necklace. She was wearing what would have been a little black dress if it had been four sizes smaller, and a summery white jacket with sleeves that stopped just below the elbow. And she wore white gloves! There was a red purse—and red shoes!

"Mrs. Bushrow!" I exclaimed. She was all that I had imagined, and a good deal more.

"Yes, my dear," she said, "I am Hattie Bushrow."

Coming into the living room, she took in everything in a brief but very efficient survey. It suddenly struck me that I was being judged.

Recalling that Harriet was an expert on antique furniture, I said, "I'm afraid it is all new."

"All furniture starts out that way," she said. Then she looked around again and added, "It is very pretty."

I felt this was faint praise but perhaps kindly meant. We sat down and she turned her attention to me. I had on light blue slacks and a matching silk blouse with a discreet monogram. I was wearing my gray mules. I knew I was in perfect taste— better taste than Harriet Bushrow, thank you. But somehow I knew she was calculating all of this. I was very nervous and uncertain of myself.

Then suddenly, she smiled, and I was completely at ease.

"Now, darlin'," she said—she has this wonderful Old South accent—"I believe you have something to tell me."

Yes, I had something to tell her, and I had rehearsed it several times, but I had not made up my mind where to begin. I said as much.

She was quite sympathetic, said she understood how hard it must be for me so recently after my husband's suicide.

"His murder," I corrected her.

She pretended to be surprised, her eyes growing large, her mouth gathered into an *O*: After a moment's pause, she said, "But the room was locked, and the police assure us that he took his own life, so why do you say it was murder?"

"Because you do," I accused. "You wouldn't be here if you did not. *You* say he did not commit suicide. And *I* say he did not commit suicide."

"I know why *I* say it. Why do *you* say it?"

Well, there it was. Why did I not think Holly had killed himself? Certainly he had never seemed inclined in that way. And when I last saw him, he appeared very confident, very self-possessed.

"I know it looks like suicide," I admitted. "And I can't offer any other explanation. But at the same time, I simply can't see Charles Hollonbrook killing himself. It wasn't his nature. That's all I can say." I paused, expecting her to make some rejoinder, but it became obvious immediately that she was waiting for me to go on. "Perhaps," I added, "it's just that I don't want it to be that way. And because—well because I very much *need* it to be murder."

"In that case," she said, "I'll lay my cards on the table and get one question out in the open and taken care of. What were you doing during that time when everybody thought you were down at Wilboro Beach—staying at Mrs. Hutton's—wasn't it? But you weren't really, were you? You weren't there on May 26th or 27th, were you?"

She looked at me—very kindly but insistently, waiting for me to explain about Wilboro Beach and May 26 to 27. "So you suspect me," I said. It was only natural that she should.

"No," she said, "I do not—not now, at any rate. If you had killed your husband, you would have been careful to be where you could receive word when his body was found. He was killed sometime after he went to bed—maybe a little after midnight. The body wasn't found until noon the next day. You could have killed him and gotten back to Mrs. Hutton's by that time—easily. But they didn't find you until the twenty-ninth. And the maid at Mrs. Hutton's says you didn't use your bed for three nights running.

"Of course, that's your private business," she continued, "but it will all come out when the sheriff discovers—when I tell him—that it was murder. You see, I have to find an explanation. You were with a man, I suppose."

Holly's death was a very real shock to me. The readers will probably think me a hypocrite for saying so. It was not that I loved him, and yet perhaps I did just a little. Loss was not the shock, though I'll explain the loss presently. The shock came when I began to view myself in a different light. I told myself I wasn't ashamed. But what I saw in myself wasn't pretty. It was more that I was surprised. I was surprised at how little feeling I had. *Cynical* was the word that came to me, and I could not escape it.

How must I appear to a woman from another age—a woman

such as Harriet Bushrow? The sexual revolution—open marriage—women's lib—what would she know about such things? She would judge me, no doubt. She might well condemn me as a "scarlet woman." That didn't bother me. But I feared that she would find me merely cynical, empty, without value.

Nevertheless, I needed Harriet Bushrow—really needed her. I believed that when she heard my story, she would become my ally.

So I began at the beginning.

I grew up in a small town in eastern North Carolina—not far from the Virginia border. It was an uptight little place—Baptist churches, Dairy Queen, all those things—not so different from Stedbury. They tell me it has changed back there. There are drugs and teenage pregnancy and all the rest. But it wasn't that way when I was a girl.

After high school, I went to Raleigh to a business college. I learned a lot in Raleigh. I was all right at the business college—top of the class, in fact. But there were other things. I found that men looked at me and that I liked it. I was very confident.

Then there was Holly with the position here in Stedbury, and I became his secretary. We didn't become lovers for over a year.

I was not the cause of the divorce. That had been coming on for several years. Linda was the girl Holly had married as a first wife.

Yes, I am cynical. I admit it. She was a first wife and that was all. Holly was on the way up, and she could not cope with that. She whined a lot and complained, and I am sure that she knew she was merely tolerated and actually rejected.

She probably did not know about me and Holly, though she should have suspected. But Holly and I were very circumspect in the office. And after all, he didn't marry me until a year after the divorce.

Meanwhile, we were together as often as we could get away

without arousing suspicion. I know all the motels at a radius of thirty miles from Stedbury.

When we were married, I knew what Holly expected of me. Sex—yes, Holly had an appetite that way. Yet there was as much ego in it as hormones. He was a dominant male animal out for conquest in an age of sexual equality. He needed it. It drove him.

Oh, I found out about that very soon. And I admit that I was hurt. I had yet to develop my carapace. I cried buckets over his first infidelity. But he was not going to let it lead to divorce. He swore he loved me. He promised that if I stayed with him, together we would have everything we wanted. He promised me jewelry—that was how I got my tennis bracelet—the first one in town. Still I was not satisfied.

Then he took out the policy on his life—half a million dollars. He asked me if that didn't show that he meant what he said.

I was still very naïve, and half a million sounded very big to me. So I began to weaken. Holly said we should have an "open marriage." Everything I read suggested that other women were doing it. So why shouldn't I? I decided to go along. Holly had a new fling about once a year. And since he always discarded the woman and was careful not to get her or me pregnant, I put my trust in that life-insurance policy.

Meanwhile, I was not a pushover. I have had only two affairs, and I was careful not to seem interested in men.

At this point, Mrs. Bushrow interrupted.

"How different it all is!" she said. "We always flirted. Our husbands expected it. Not serious flirting—just polite banter. If men found us attractive, in a nice way, of course, it showed the world our husbands had won a prize when they married us. We flirted, but we never had affairs."

I realized that this woman from another age was not surprised at what I had told her. "You are not shocked! You do not judge me, do you?"

"No, I'm not shocked. But I do judge you," she replied. "I judge all you modern girls. You have sold your birthright for a mess of pottage. In my day, we managed our husbands. They worked for us. And we worked for them, too. We kept the home and had their children. And we helped them in their careers. But you see, we fascinated them. We kept them charmed. And we were true to them. It would have been heartless if we hadn't been.

"Yes, I judge you. But then you didn't have the training we had, and that's not your fault."

"I am not proud of myself," I said, "but it's not because I was unfaithful to Holly. For I was faithful to him. I was faithful to him as long as he was faithful to me." And then I got on with my story.

Holly's latest interest was Kim Mayburn. She is a divorcée who came back here a little over a year ago. Her father was the state senator from this district for many years. I think it gave Holly a kick to think he was bedding a senator's daughter.

So, about that time Clifford Avery came along—from Baltimore—Ivy League—very suave and good-looking—self-assured—all the things Holly would have liked to be if he could have. And Cliff liked what he saw in me. I met him in Louisville at the Derby. We amused each other and finally fell into his bed.

"If you want to know where I was on the night of May 26," I said, "I was on a yacht with Cliff; and if his word is not enough, then I have no alibi." I paused, and Mrs. Bushrow seemed to be considering this.

I resumed my explanation.

After Holly's funeral, Dan Blake, my lawyer, and I opened Holly's bank box. It was jammed with all the stuff that might be expected—birth certificate, his medals, papers of all sorts, fire insurance, and so on. We found the policy made out to me as beneficiary; it had been in effect since 1981. But we had not expected another policy for $500,000 made out to the benefit of Kimberlin Mayburn. For a minute or two, I was stunned. It was humiliating and unfair after all I had put up with. And then it just hurt. I couldn't keep the tears back, and I'm afraid I was hysterical.

Poor Dan! There we were in the bank vault together. It must have been embarrassing for him. He is such a nice little man with a nice little wife and four children! And then after I calmed down, he pointed out that we had not found the will.

It was just as if a great dark cloud was hovering over me. I didn't know just what it meant, but I felt that a will absolutely had to be found. Yet I knew Chuck well enough that I was confident the will, if there was one, would have been in that box.

Dan and I went immediately to Holly's office, and with Paula Stout, Holly's secretary, we went through every file, every drawer, absolutely everything in the office. Then we came out to the house and went through everything here.

"Who was the lawyer that drew up the will?" Dan asked.

"Wasn't it you?" I asked.

"No."

I was positive that Holly had never gone to any lawyer other than Dan.

"Then there is no will, is there?"

"It begins to look that way," he said.

"But what happens if there is no will?"

"The statutes of North Carolina take effect. There will be distribution among the heirs at law."

"And they are?"

"Yourself and Holly's children."

That was when the real panic set in. Holly had always been reckless. When he got money, he spent it—clothes, cars, our house. And he was reckless with credit, too. When he began developing Hollondale Estates, he plunged pretty deeply. I did not know how far. But in the bank box, we had found note after note—all owed to the Estonia Savings and Loan. The obligations were all in the name of Hollonbrook Realty, Inc., or Hollondale

Estates, Inc. But if all those notes were foreclosed, Holly's personal estate would amount to his checking account and the residence, and there is still a lien on that.

My Porsche is in my name, and I have some jewelry and a few furs. Whatever may be left over after Holly's debts are settled would be divided four ways. And I would have practically nothing from that.

And, the life insurance won't pay off in case of suicide!

That was my story, and that was why I was staking everything on Mrs. Bushrow's ability to prove that Chuck died, not by his own hand but at the hands of a murderer.

"Darling," Mrs. Bushrow said after she had considered this a little while, "with your husband out of the picture, are you going to marry this Mr. Avery, I think you said his name was?"

I took a deep breath. "There is no marriage for me in this," I said.

"Why not? You speak of this gentleman's cultivation and good looks. And a man with a yacht—and I must say, sweetheart, you seem to have thought him ideal. Is there something I am missing?"

"You are missing something," I admitted. "He has a wife, and the money is hers. Cliff is strongly attracted to me, but he could never live without money—lots of money."

"Well, dear," my visitor said regretfully, "if an old woman can say so, you seem to have driven your ducks to a mighty poor market."

"To put it mildly," I added.

"Don't worry about that now," she said. "It was murder, all right; we are going to prove it."

There was one more thing that I had for Mrs. Bushrow, and I placed an envelope in her hand.

From this point on, Mrs. Bushrow became the dominant party in our interview. Consequently, it seems better to turn the narrative over to her.

NEW LIGHT
ON THE MYSTERY

>> Harriet Bushrow <<

That was quite a story Alice told me—all that about "open marriage" and the missing will and the insurance policy. She just told it all, and I have to hand it to her—she was very frank. Then, after she got through with her other revelations, she put a brown envelope into my hand.

"This was in the bank box," she said.

Out of the envelope, I drew a yellowed newspaper clipping. It was from the Roanoke, Virginia, paper, dated April 10, 1971. There was a picture of a woman—about like most pictures in the papers. The story said: KITTY HERBERT RELEASED FROM PEN. "Kitty Cornelia Herbert, who was convicted of the stabbing death of her husband, the late J. H. Herbert, in 1959, has been released from Beckwith Prison for Women after having served nine years of a twenty-year sentence. The public will remember that Herbert was found guilty on all charges but pleaded extenuating circumstances, testifying that James Howard Herbert, the murdered man, had habitually forced her to engage in demeaning and dangerous sex acts. Because of the husband's position as justice of the peace in Hainsford County, the case received wide notice." In the margin was penciled "Caroline Rawlings."

I couldn't see what this had to do with anything, and my brain was just full of so many other things that I just had to know about. So I merely put the clipping back into the envelope and laid it on the little lamp table beside me while my mind went on to other things.

No will! That meant that good old Holly's children were involved. Whether or not there was a will, surely they would expect something to come to them. Would they have known that their father was in debt and that there wasn't much estate for them to inherit? From the looks of things—Hollondale Estates, you see, and being on the board of the country club, and district governor—I didn't have any trouble imagining how someone on the outside would get the idea that Charles Hollonbrook had left an estate like the Big Rock Candy Mountain.

So I asked.

"Tell me about that first wife and the children."

Alice made an ugly face that put me into the picture but didn't give me any of the details.

"Holly has taken a lot of criticism from them—and it is all unfair."

"I suppose he paid support?"

"Yes, regularly without fail."

"I understand the mother has exclusive custody."

"No, it wasn't that way," Alice said. "Right after the divorce, Holly had no way to take care of the children. So he left them with Linda. And she was agreeable. Then when we got married, he decided to exercise his rights and tried having Jimmy, the oldest—the other two are girls—spend the summer with us. I did everything I knew to be, if not a second mother, at least a friend. Jimmy was belligerent and stubborn, and Holly was afraid to punish him because the boy was so high-strung.

"The second summer, he came and stayed a week. Linda had stuffed his head with so many lies about Holly and me that we couldn't do a thing with the boy. When he hit his father on the nose with a junior baseball bat, Holly sent him back to his mother.

"She has made a real mess of him. The school notified Holly that Jimmy was on pot, and Holly raised a stink with Linda about that. She denied it. And that's pretty much where we left it. Then last year, Jimmy wanted to go to State, and Holly gave him the money. But Jimmy failed all his courses the first semester. So he came home and wanted money to go to California to study something about television. Holly said NO in big capitals, and they actually had a fight. Now Linda has told everyone that Holly refused to help Jimmy."

"Aha!" I said. "When did this fight happen?"

"About the end of March."

"Was that the last time he was in the house?"

"Well, no," she said. "As a matter of fact, he came back a week or two later whining and halfway apologizing. This time, he wanted money to get his car out of the pound. . . . Oh, yes, his father bought him the car, but he said Jimmy would just have to work to get the money to get it out of the pound."

Well, I found all of that interesting. "How long was Jimmy in the house at that time?"

"Why, I don't know," she said. "An hour—hour and a half. I could hear him arguing with Holly from the bedroom where I was reading."

"Where did your husband keep his guns?" was my next question.

"Oh my God, I never thought of that! You don't think . . ."

I waited for her to complete her question. During the pause, I could see her adjusting to the idea.

"I see what you mean. Jimmy was an heir. But would he go that far?"

"Oh, my dear," I said, "with all this television, these young people get to hear and see about everything, and I'm just old-fashioned enough to say, 'Monkey see, monkey do.' "

"But he would have no way of knowing there was no will."

"Wouldn't need to," I said. "He's his father's son. He would expect to get something from his father's estate, will or no will. And even if you told him, he would never be able to understand that his father was financially strapped. Now the guns. Where did your husband keep them?"

They were in the basement, but she said that Charles had kept them locked up. I asked if I could have a look, and she said I could. So we went down some steep stairs from the kitchen. And when we got down to the basement, there was a regular shooting range down there with special lights trained on the targets. It was just elaborate.

"He planned this house around his pistol range," Alice said. "That's why the house is so broad across the front. He had his pistol-club buddies come down here once a week. They shot away for more than an hour sometimes. That's why I made Holly use silencers."

And that explained something that had been troubling me from the very start.

There were rifles locked in a regular gun cabinet with a glass door, and beneath that there were locked drawers for the pistols.

"And where are the keys kept?" I asked.

"In a drawer in Holly's bedroom."

"And you were in your bedroom when the boy was last here?"

"Yes."

"Reading?"

"Yes—reading and talking on the phone."

"Is your bedroom closer to the living room than your husband's?"

"Yes, it is."

"And would the boy have to pass your door to get to his father's bedroom?"

"Yes."

"And was the door open?"

"I believe it was."

"Would you have seen the boy if he passed your door?"

Well, it turned out that she wouldn't have seen him because the head of her bed, where she was reading, was against the wall where the door was. So it was plain as day that the boy could have gotten the pistol, ammunition, and silencer. Whether he would know when his father was going to be in Borderville or not, I couldn't say. But perhaps that would come out later.

"Now I want to know about the house key. Where do you keep it?" I asked.

"I keep mine in my purse, and Holly kept his on his key ring. Martha comes once a week and has her own key," she explained, "and, oh yes, Paula."

"Paula?"

"Paula Stout. She's Holly's secretary. She feeds the dog when both of us are gone."

Now I'm a back number, and I am the first to say so, but I have read about all the things that cause feminists to complain—that now secretaries won't make the coffee and won't do this and won't do that. So naturally I raised my eyebrows at a secretary who fed the dog.

"Oh, Paula took care of everything when both of us were gone. She's been in the office ever since I left it."

So this Paula was in a position to know that Charles Hollonbrook was going to be in Borderville on May 26 to 27 and probably made the reservation at the Borderville Inn. And she knew Alice would be away—probably even knew why—and with the run of the house she could undoubtedly find the key to the drawers where the pistols were kept. I took my little memorandum book out of my purse and put a line under Paula's name.

"Now, where can I find her?" I asked.

"At the office. She's running the office. Or she might be at one of the Ducky's. We have three franchise shops—Ducky's, you know—the food shops. Franks, hamburgers, and sausage biscuits. With the real estate as slow as it has been, it has been very good to have Ducky's. Paula kept up with them for us when Holly was away."

I wondered if those shops and the people who worked there might be something to look into. How many people we deal with daily whom we may offend—perhaps more seriously than we know! But just then I wanted to know about Paula Stout. Had she been another of Charles Hollonbrook's conquests?

So I asked.

"Well—" Alice said. "With Holly, it would not be out of line to think so. I have wondered about it myself. After all, he had it on with me when I was just what she is. So why not Paula? I finally decided no, there is nothing there."

Nothing there? The way she said it left a question in my mind. And it seemed to me I had to know more about this young person who had a key and knew where the victim was going to be and when he would be there.

"Is this Paula unmarried?" I inquired.

"Yes, unmarried."

"How old?"

"About thirty-five."

"Does she go out with anybody?"

"No boyfriend—that's what you mean, isn't it?"

Well, yes, that was what I meant. I got the impression that Alice took Paula for an old maid.

"Now, darling," I said, "you have to tell me everything if you want me to find the killer. Why don't you think Paula had a fling with your husband?"

"Because she adored him. She has adored him for more than ten years. Holly could never be faithful to a woman for three years, let alone ten. So—they've never been to bed. At least I don't think they have. Besides, she is a Baptist."

I don't know how Baptists get the reputation for being so

holy. Aren't they the ones that are always having to go down to the front of the church to "get right with God"? Well, if they have to get "right with God," doesn't that mean they sometimes get "wrong with God"?

But I wrote down *Baptist* by Paula's name. And Maud is a Baptist. I was pretty sure Maud would have an opinion about Miss Stout.

"Now, let's see," I said. "Going back to the gun club. They met once a week. Did they meet just the same when you and Mr. Hollonbrook were away?"

They did.

Then how did they get in?

It turned out that each of them had a key to the basement door. Alice led me through the furnace room and showed me the door.

"I believe you don't have neighbors on either side," I said.

"That's right."

"So any one of those men could get into the house without anybody seeing him and get the gun—but he wouldn't have a key to the drawers, would he?"

"No. Those are only Holly's guns in the drawers," Alice said.

"But one of them could search through the house and find the key, couldn't he?"

"Well, no," she answered. "When I go away, I always lock the door at the top of the stairs."

"Maybe Paula could have unlocked it," I suggested.

"But why would she come down here? There was no need for it."

That was true—at least we did not know of a reason—unless she took the gun herself. But if she didn't take the gun and didn't unlock the door at the top of the stairs, the men in the pistol-shooting club could not have gotten the Hollonbrook gun without breaking the drawer open. And the drawer showed no sign of having been forced.

I will admit that it looked impossible. A man was shot in a

locked room with his own gun—that had been locked in his basement at home. And the key to that drawer was upstairs, and the door between the basement and the upstairs was locked.

It looked as though the men of the pistol club were out of it. Paula and the boy, Jim, could have gotten the gun, and Paula was in the best position to know about Charles Hollonbrook's movements, while Jimmy was angry with his father. He could have got the key to the drawer—but no! He did not have the key to the house.

"You had a key," I said, "your husband had a key to the house, and Miss Stout had another. What about the key to the door at the top of the stairs to the basement? Where was it kept?"

"It is always in the lock on the inside of the door."

"And was it left in the lock when the door was locked?"

"Yes, it was."

Then it would be impossible to go from the basement upstairs when the door was locked, even if the intruder had a key.

"I suppose the gun club would know when your husband was not planning to be in town," I said.

"I really don't know," she replied. "I suppose they would."

We had come back upstairs and Alice had gone into the kitchen to get us some coffee. I took the opportunity to go through the house—said I was going to use the powder room, but really I just wanted to see the house. There wasn't a stick of furniture in it that I would have wanted if you gave it to me—all modern—selected, I imagine, by a decorator and very expensive. All in good taste. But impersonal. That was the word: *impersonal.* With all the wonderful things that people can have nowadays, it seems to me that they are often very impersonal— no continuity. There was Charles Hollonbrook going from one woman to another. Nothing personal there. And dear little Alice, whatever she had been before she got together with Hollonbrook, he had made her life impersonal. Impersonal people living in an impersonal house with an impersonal marriage. But the personal will break through. It's like lava inside the mountain. The cold exterior can hold it only so long.

Back in the living room with our cups of impersonal instant coffee and our impersonal Pepperidge Farm cookies, I asked Alice about the first Mrs. Hollonbrook. Had there been any recent friction there?

Only about the children.

"It isn't as though Chuck has not supported them," Alice said. "More than supported them. And if they were just a little grateful, he would have given them anything they wanted."

"Let's see," I said, "I believe I was told there were two girls. Tell me about them."

"One is eighteen, and the other is fifteen," she replied. "They would soon have expected Chuck to shell out the money to go to an expensive college, though neither one of them would have the grades to get into a really good school."

"Are they often here at the house?"

"Oh no." Alice was very definite about that. "Their mother has poisoned them against me."

"Eighteen and fifteen," I mused. "The youngest must have been little more than a baby when the divorce broke up the family."

Alice bridled just a bit at that. And I liked her better because of it. Whether she broke up the marriage or did not break up the marriage—that was her version, you see—she was uncomfortable with the way I had stated it. There was just a little conscience there.

My ways are the old ways, and I don't care who knows it. When I was a girl, there might as well have been a picket fence around me, the way I was protected. And don't think I wasn't rebellious. I gave my parents many an anxious moment. But the man I wanted and got was Lamar, and he was such a darling. I could never even look at another man. And he just better not have looked at another woman.

So there was Linda. And Maud said Linda talked about how she had been mistreated, while Alice said that Linda's constant nagging had broken up the marriage. What kind of woman was Linda? Could she have been behind the murder? Wasn't that the way it was in that poem about Edward that I had to learn back there at Catawba Hall? It was one of my elocution readings. Nobody nowadays even knows what an elocution reading is.

Why does your brand sae drap wi bluid
Edward, Edward . . . ?

I think it was supposed to be up in the Highlands over in Scotland. Miss Langrock said it was an ideal piece for me to read. Thought I was bloodthirsty, I suppose. Anyhow, at the end of the poem, come to find out, the mother sent Edward out to kill his daddy. I guess that kind of thing has been going on for a long time.

But Edward didn't sneak around and make it look like suicide. And Jimmy Boy did not sound to me like a young man who could pull a thing like that off even if his mother gave him a map of how to do it. Or did he? Sometimes people who don't seem to have it—you know what I mean—are pretty sneaky and can do on the sly things you wouldn't think they could do.

Well, I was sitting there. And my cup was empty, and I had eaten my cookies. And I had a few more things I needed to talk about.

I said, "Since Miss Stout is in your employ still and was your husband's secretary, I would like very much for her to give me a list of people she may know of who would have known that Mr. Hollonbrook would be in Borderville on May twenty-six to twenty-seven. Would you please ask her to do that for me?"

Of course Mrs. Hollonbrook agreed to do as I asked.

"And while you are at it," I added, "ask her where she was and what she was doing on that night. Say that we are checking the activities of everyone in Stedbury who knew where Mr. Hollonbrook was at that time." Which, of course, was true.

Alice agreed to that, too.

"Now darling," I proceeded, "do you by any chance happen to remember the date on the policy your husband took out on this other woman? I think you said Mayburn."

"February 1." From the way she answered so quickly, I could see that the poor child's mind was running in the same direction mine was.

"And the other policy—the one for you—it was still in effect. Do you know when your husband made the last payment on it?"

The answer came just as quickly. "December twenty-nine."

To me that looked like Charles Hollonbrook decided between December 29 and February 1 that he was interested in a second divorce. But I didn't discuss it with Alice.

"And the other thing is," I said, "this clipping." I picked up the envelope with the clipping from the table where I had laid it when we went downstairs. "Are you intending to give it to me?"

She nodded.

"Do you know who this Kitty Herbert is?"

"Never heard of her."

"Or Caroline Rawlings?"

"No. The clipping is a complete mystery to me. Hainsford, the place where the Herbert woman murdered her husband, was Holly's hometown, which might be reason enough for his interest in the story, but not enough to explain why he kept it in a brown envelope in the bank box."

I had to agree: But whether the clipping was connected with Hollonbrook's death, I was not prepared to say.

As you can see, I had had a very interesting interview with the young lady. A lot of good stuff, as you might say, had just fallen into my lap.

I thanked Alice for the coffee and cookies and told her, "Now, darling, don't you worry," and that sort of thing. Then I told her I wanted to see the dog before I left. So we went to the back door, and I saw that the backyard was enclosed in a chain-link fence and saw where the steps went down to the basement. There was no other house in sight. I didn't know whether that would be important or not.

It is a sweet dog—cocker spaniel.

Now you have to understand one thing. I am a truthful woman except when I want to tell a fib. But if I make a promise, I always stick by it. A little later on in this book, as you will see, I made a promise. I said I wouldn't reveal certain things.

Now how could I write the book and keep the secret? I took my problem to Professor Landrum. He is a Rotarian—senior active—and before he retired he taught English for many years at the college here in Borderville. I asked him, "What must I do?" And he said, "Mrs. Bushrow, there is no problem at all here." Then he explained.

It seems there is something called a roman à clef. I had to look it up to spell it. It is in the dictionary, all right, and it means just what he said. It's a novel about things that really happened, but all the names are changed.

So I am changing certain of the names in this book. Kitty Herbert is not the real name, and Caroline Rawlings is not her real name. And none of the names that are connected with her are real. But the rest of the story is all true.

And Professor Landrum told me something else I didn't know. He said detective stories are classical. I don't understand literary terms like that. All the same, it is impressive to know that detective stories are classical because they have a beginning, a middle, and an end.

While I don't know how a story can fail to have a beginning, a middle, and an end, I *did* understand what Professor Landrum meant when he explained that whatever has happened up to the time when the crime takes place settles what happens all the rest of the way until the mystery is solved. Then he said that the middle is the part where everything is developing and confused.

I can tell you right now: This is the middle of the Rotary Club Mystery, because I was confused. I had several notions—quite a few. And some of them turned out to be right. But there was one piece of information that I didn't even know enough about to ask for it. But it wasn't on the horizon yet, and you'll just have to wait for it.

THE BAKER STREET IRREGULARS

>> *Henry Delaporte* <<

Just before President Gene struck the bell to close our meeting—I think it was the second meeting in June—he said, "Fred Middleton would like to see—whatever he calls the bunch." He got a laugh from the club, then went on: "The detectives—the ones looking into . . ."

When he seemed at a loss to describe the group, Melvin Benson said, "You mean the Baker Street Irregulars, Gene."

As we all know, the real Baker Street Irregulars were the London urchins who scurried around and ferreted out information for Sherlock Holmes. It happened that one of the television networks had recently been featuring a series about the adventures of Holmes and Dr. Watson. Everyone laughed. And those of us who were following Mrs. Bushrow's progress—I might say, with a good deal of interest—were the "Baker Street Irregulars" from then on.

About fifteen of us stayed on after Gene had rung the bell and dismissed the club.

The reason Fred wanted to see us was that he had received

in the morning mail a letter from Harriet Bushrow, and it raised some questions he thought we should consider. The letter was as follows:

Dear Fred,

Here I am at the above address staying with my dear old friend Maud Bradfield. I have a lovely room, and Maud showers me with every attention. If I didn't have to do any detective work, this would be about the pleasantest vacation a person could desire.

Which brings me to the thing I want you to think about.

Fred, I am finding a lot of things about Charles Hollonbrook that do not reflect credit on Rotary. Now you and I know how fine at least ninety-nine percent of the Rotarians really are. But we also know that there are people out there—writers and so on—who make snide remarks about Rotary—want us to think Rotarians are "operators" just grubbing for money and that sort of thing.

Well, I have to admit that your Charles Hollonbrook was an operator. Fred, I'm finding things about your district governor that, if they are brought out, will embarrass Rotary plenty—or at least they ought to.

I give the man credit—he came up in a hurry, but on the way up he did some pretty mean things to a good many people. He was a womanizer, and there are other little peccadilloes. So your friends should be thinking about whether they want me to go on with this—because what I find is bound to give Rotary a black eye.

On the other side of the question, I am as certain as can be that your Mr. Hollonbrook was murdered;

and I don't suppose we can let a thing like that go without trying to bring whoever did it to justice, can we?

I leave it up to the Rotarians. It is their club, and I'll quit what I'm doing and go home if that's what they want.

Give my love to Daisy Beth.

Faithfully yours,
Harriet Gardner Bushrow

When Fred had finished reading the letter, the reaction of the Irregulars was nothing at all. After a minute or more, Fred prompted us: "What do you think?"

"What do I think?" Keith said. (That's Keith Duncan.) "I think our district governor got his tail caught."

"It sure looks like it," Leon Jones agreed.

"The question is what we are going to do about it," Fred observed.

"Apply the Four-Way Test." This suggestion came from Milt Powell.

There was a pause before Trajan McDowell said, "In what way? I mean, how does the Four-Way Test apply to a case like this?"

The Four-Way Test is a kind of totem of Rotary. It asks four questions. First: Is it the truth? Second: Is it fair to all concerned? Third: Will it build goodwill and better friendships? And fourth: Will it be beneficial to all concerned?

"All right," Leon said, "is it the truth?" citing the first test.

There it was. If Harriet Bushrow said it, there wasn't one of us who didn't think it was the truth. Right there in our own club, I could think of three members who had been up to the sort of thing Mrs. Bushrow's letter suggested. Who would deny that the same could be true of the district governor?

Next, was it fair to all concerned? That one had us stumped. If Mrs. Bushrow succeeded in finding the culprit, everything was bound to come out. It would be in all the papers. Rotary would look bad, and it was sure to embarrass Hollonbrook's friends and family. Was that being fair to all?

Fred made the point that if a man had been murdered, it was unfair to him if the killer did not come to justice.

"But what makes you so sure old Charles Hollonbrook would want everything to hang out?" Trajan objected; and we all had to admit that a dead man should be allowed to rest in peace.

As far as the next test went—would it build goodwill and friendships—nobody saw how that could apply. And the fourth test—would it be beneficial to all concerned—was a sure loser. It could not benefit Charles Hollonbrook. A scandal would not be beneficial to Rotary. And it certainly would not benefit the murderer.

I think we were about ready to call it quits and ask Mrs. Bushrow to come home, when Leon said, "What do you suppose that old boy was up to, anyhow?"

"Yeah," Keith agreed. "I want to know what he did."

Suddenly, the mood of the group had swung 180 degrees. We were all for going on with the investigation. At that point, J. L. Garrison, a senior active—the typical gentleman of an older generation, who is also something of a character—suddenly declaimed, "Fiat justitia, ruat caelum! Let justice be done though the sky falls."

That settled the matter. We told Fred to instruct Mrs. Bushrow to go on with what she was doing and to assure her that we would support her in all her expenses and in every other way possible.

AT THE BAPTIST CHURCH WITH MAUD

>> Harriet Bushrow <<

Gossip has a bad reputation. But as a means of clearing the mind and stimulating thought, I find it most effective. The trouble with gossip is that most people consider it an end in itself: But when it is taken as a means of forming the opinion and rising above ignorance, it has great usefulness in society. What is journalism but a kind of gossip—not as good or as useful as the back-fence variety—because there is no give-and-take except maybe in the letters from the readers. And even when we watch the evening discussion of the news on TV, we don't gain the full benefit of gossip because we don't get to put in *our* two cents worth.

What I am getting around to is that Maud and I have been girlfriends for over seventy years, and there is nobody with whom I would rather gossip. Why, gossip is about the only intellectual activity left for old ladies like me, and without it our poor old brains would dry up and blow away. When a woman gives up gossip, she might as well be dead.

So as soon as I got to the house, Maud said, "Now lunch is ready, and I'm dying to hear."

That darling girl had made a delicious salmon salad—served

it on crisp, fresh lettuce—and with rolls and ice tea, it made just a perfect lunch.

Maud was as interested as could be in what I had to tell her.

"Well," she said when I got to the end of my story, "I guess that lets the widow out. A half million dollars sounds like a pretty good alibi to me."

"Yes," I agreed, looking out the window at Maud's mock orange. Across the street, a little dog ran out and barked at a passing car. "That," I went on, "and the fact that now she is—don't you know—actually encouraging me to find out who did it."

The little dog kept on barking—proud of itself, I suppose. It made me think of Alice Hollonbrook's little cocker and the fact that Miss Stout had a key to the house so she could feed the dog.

"Now Maud, I want your opinion on Miss Paula Stout. She goes to your church, so you are bound to know her," I said.

"Know her?" Maud replied. "That poor child! She's so good, she makes a pest of herself."

Now you see what I mean about gossip. It's very illuminating. It cuts right through to the meat of the matter.

"So good that she is a pest." Surely you have known somebody on that order. A meek little thing that is all the things the Bible says you ought to be—so good! And knows it, too! The thing I like best about Our Lord is the way he saw through people like that.

Maud said she thought the trouble with Paula was that she was plain, while her sister was beautiful.

"Yes," she said, "Roberta, the older sister, entered beauty contests, though I don't remember if she won any of them— you'd think I'd remember. But she attracted men like flies to molasses. And that left poor Paula with nothing but good works to fall back on."

I don't have much to say for psychiatrists and analysts and people who tell you all your troubles stem from your mother's shutting you in a closet for ten minutes when you were four years old. But I do know that lots of girls with beautiful sisters will do anything to get equal attention. And, of course, if the sisters hadn't been so pretty, the ugly ones wouldn't have known how much attention one girl can get.

Maud told me about a friend who had flu last winter. This Paula found out about it and brought chicken broth—kept bringing it. Well, a person gets tired of chicken broth after a certain time. And it seems this do-gooder is always volunteering to be coordinator or chairman of some project—like dressing the dolls at Christmas for the Salvation Army. Then she just keeps urging more and more dolls on everybody and specifies in great detail how the doll clothes are to be made. I recognized the type. Yes indeed!

So after our conversation, I was very interested in Miss Paula Stout. That's when Maud said we'd see her in church and no doubt Paula would put on her act for us.

"Oh, she's very popular," Maud declared with a drop or two of vinegar in her voice, "with little old ladies."

Maud's church is about as old as I am—which is just the way a church building ought to be. Outside, it is red brick with white columns and steps leading up to the door. Inside, somebody has painted the walls pale green, which was the wrong thing to do. There is a large stained-glass window on the right—the woman at the well—and on the left another big window of Christ at Gethsemane. Behind the choir is the baptistry with the Jordan River in stained glass and a light behind it.

Whatever else you may say about the Baptists, they are true to themselves; I have to hand it to them.

The woodwork is dark oak. The pews are curved so as to surround the podium, which projects out into the room. That was just fine for me because it makes it possible to look over and see part of the congregation on the other side.

When Maud and I came up from attending her class, which

was in the basement of the Sunday-school annex, the organist, in her light gray robe, was just entering, clutching her music. Pretty soon, she had it all spread out on the organ and began to play.

People were coming in from all directions, exchanging greetings. Baptists do a lot more of that sort of thing than I am accustomed to. After all, we Presbyterians have to keep up our reputation as God's frozen people.

Well, we were sitting there in all that hubbub when Maud leaned over to me and said, "There she is now—standing just where nobody can get around her."

I looked kitty-cornered across the auditorium and saw this little thing in a little straight black-and-white checked skirt and a black jacket with some kind of red pin on the lapel. Mouse-colored hair—straight, bobbed, and combed behind her ears. She had this round face and not too bad a figure—a tiny bit on the plump side—"pneumatic," Lamar used to call it. She was talking to a lady apparently in her fifties and was holding up all the people who were trying to get by. Finally, somebody pushed her. She turned to him with an obvious, radiant smile.

"Turning the other cheek," Maud whispered.

"You don't like her, do you?"

"Lord, no!" she replied.

Maud tries to be a good Baptist, and if she doesn't make it, it really isn't her fault. She is pure gold—I wouldn't want you to think anything else—but she never did quite fit the mold. When we were in school, Maud played cards, and that was long before Baptist ladies had anything to do with cards.

"Look at her now," Maud said.

Paula had progressed about twenty feet into the room and was leaning over the front pew, talking past the heads of people in the second pew to a ghostly little lady on the third row.

"That's Pearl Travis she is talking to," Maud explained. "Pearl lost her sister recently."

I have to admit that the Baptist religion is enjoyable. The

service is always fun. Baptist ministers tell stories that make the congregation laugh—and other stories that are pitiful and plead with you to respond in a sympathetic way. If there ever was any starch in those Baptists, it's all gone by the time the service is over and the congregation has had a complete emotional workout.

When the last hymn was sung and the benediction had been pronounced, Maud said, "Come on. I'll introduce you."

We pushed through the crowd slowly because everyone spoke to Maud and she had to introduce me. Finally, we reached the quarry. Paula turned as Maud called her name. She had her Bible and Sunday-school book in one hand and her purse in the other. There was a certain amount of juggling of these three objects before her right hand was stretched out to me.

"Mrs. Bushrow!" the child said. She was no more than five foot two or three. "I am so glad to see you. I want to tell you what a comfort your visit has been to poor Mrs. Hollonbrook. Alice, Mrs. Hollonbrook, spoke to me yesterday and explained that she was not satisfied to think that Mr. Hollonbrook took his own life—such a sad thing—and said you were being so helpful. I do appreciate anything you can do for her."

I had not expected little Miss Goody Two-Shoes to be so socially effective.

"Of course, I would do anything in the world to help her," she continued.

I didn't know how much Alice Hollonbrook had told this woman about me, but this was one of those times when it might be just as well if she thought I was a batty old thing. I suppose some people might say I wouldn't find it hard to give that impression.

I held Paula's hand and said, "Darling, she told me how thoughtful you have been—and so sweet. Oh, I know at a time like this how important it is to have thoughtful friends."

"Were you acquainted with either Mr. Hollonbrook or Mrs.

Hollonbrook before this tragedy?'' she inquired. And it sounded a bit as though she was asking me for my credentials.

"Oh, no,'' I said. "But, don't you see, it happened right there in my own town—Borderville—and my late husband was such a prominent Rotarian—why, I just couldn't be here in town—I'm visiting my friend here—old school chum—and I felt it was just a duty to visit that poor woman.''

Was I laying it on too thick? I must have been, for Paula Stout countered with: "I understood you are the one who wanted to know where I was on the night of May 26, and a list of all who knew where Mr. Hollonbrook was at that time.'' She said it rather coldly. When she did not put on her sanctified smile, her face was like a mask.

"I have typed it all out,'' Paula continued. "It's here in my purse. I was going to drop it off to Alice on the way home from church. I'll just give it to you now.''

Again there was a rearrangement of the Bible, Sunday-school quarterly, and her purse, and in due time she pulled out a folded piece of paper.

"Oh, that is so good of you,'' I gushed. "Of course there is no reason to suspect you at all. But they always collect alibis, don't they? In detective stories, you know. And so I said to that sweet Alice Hollonbrook, 'Dear, you must collect all the alibis—just from everyone, you see.''

I took the paper.

"So sweet of you to do this!'' I said. "But then a little bird tells me that this is the kind of person you are.''

We were hardly out of the church before Maud told me what a hypocrite I am. Said I was getting worse as the years go by. I expect she's right. But she was almost laughing as she said it. Meanwhile, I was dying to see what was written on that paper. As soon as I got to the car, I unfolded the missive and read:

> On Monday, May 26, I worked in the office ar-
> ranging for the plumber to fix a leak at the Ducky's

in Eunice. I made out checks, paid the bills for all three Ducky's locations, and posted same in the account book. I showed two houses, made out the ad to be included in Wednesday's *Gazette,* and sent flowers in Mr. Hollonbrook's name to the opening of the new Stedbury Children's Clinic, which is in one of our properties. At 5:30, I picked up Mrs. Rose Moody from McMenamee's Rest Home (her seventy-sixth birthday)—took her to my house for dinner. She stayed with me through the night, and I took her back to the rest home after breakfast on the 27th.

People who knew where Mr. Hollonbrook was on May 26: Jeff Sandifer, president of Stedbury Rotary Club. Everett Greenwood, secretary-treasurer, Stedbury Rotary Club. Francis Duff, rector of St. Barnabas Episcopal Church. Gene Spencer, president, Borderville Rotary Club. Jody Russell, secretary-treasurer, Borderville Rotary Club. Frank Nicholson. Jimmy Hollonbrook.

Well, that was interesting. I wondered whether there might not be one or two others who knew of Chuck Hollonbrook's whereabouts on that night.

I CALL ON
MRS. LINDA HOLLONBROOK

>> Harriet Bushrow <<

I am tired of the Rotary Club Mystery. Oh, I adored the detective part of it. That's just fun and exciting, and for an old lady it is better than a shot of gin. It gets me out of the house and in this case even out of town; and if it doesn't exactly revive the flesh, it revives the mind, so that I feel fifteen years younger.

Ha! Even at that, I would be seventy-three.

The part I don't like is all this writing. When they insisted I must write up my part of the Famous DAR Mystery, I should have said *no*! And now I have this plagued business about the Hollonbrook murder to write up. Oh well, maybe I'll be dead by the time the next mystery comes along.

But to get on with it, Maud and I chewed over the names on Paula Stout's list.

The name of Frank Nicholson was new to me. But when I asked Maud about it, she laughed and said, "There's nothing there," and I asked why.

"Because he's a jeweler. I've known him for years. He didn't deal in antique stuff: But when I had my silver collection, he was always asking if I had added anything to it. He really knows quite a lot about old silver, and he helped me sell the collection after Jay died."

"But why would he want to know the whereabouts of Charles Hollonbrook?" I wanted to know.

"I'll ask him." Maud picked up the phone and called the man. There had been something about the lease on his shop that he wanted to talk about with Hollonbrook personally.

So I crossed Nicholson off the list as harmless, along with the Episcopal rector.

And those Rotarians—I just hadn't thought about it, but every last Rotarian in Borderville had known when Charles Hollonbrook would be in town. They would have been notified and reminded—reminded for a month at least—so that there would be a good attendance for the glorious district governor.

Now I wouldn't like to think of Rotarians committing murder, but all the same—I know Lamar Bushrow, that old darling—of course it never would have happened, but Lamar would have come mighty close to killing any man who made improper advances to me.

So with all those Rotarians in Borderville, if there was one who had some connection with Stedbury, North Carolina— well, there might be something. Or again, there is the annual weekend at the Greenbriar when the Rotarians get together. And there could be more than one of the Borderville Rotarians up there with pretty young wives. And if Chuck Hollonbrook went off to the Greenbriar, that would be such an opportunity for Alice Hollonbrook to go off with her sweetie from Baltimore. And suppose that good old Chuck Hollonbrook started something last year at the Greenbriar and wanted to continue it at the Borderville Inn!

You see, you could imagine all sorts of ways to explain how a Borderville Rotarian would have a motive. I began to think that perhaps I ought to write to Henry Delaporte or Fred or somebody else in Borderville and alert them to see if they could find out something along those lines.

But that was beside the point just at this time. What I needed to do was right there in Stedbury.

There is no way an eighty-eight-year-old woman can get very much out of a boy of nineteen. I couldn't get anything out of my own son when he was that age. And specially if the boy had anything to do with his father's death, there would be no chance to get him to talk in any way that might tell me something. But perhaps the mother would be a different matter. And if the boy was involved, I was pretty sure the mother would be involved, too. Any way I looked at it, I wanted to talk to Charles Hollonbrook's first wife.

So I looked in the phone book and found Linda Hollonbrook at 619 Mountain View Drive. Maud told me how to get there. Just before I left about ten o'clock Monday morning to see what I could do, I said to Maud, "Now, darling, don't be surprised if I sound crazy when I call you in a little bit. Just hold the phone and don't say anything until I hang up."

Of course, it was a long time ago, but it seemed to me that Lamar junior, when he got his first old car, could make it backfire by turning off the ignition and then turning it back on right quick. I could hear that old thing going *bang bang,* and I would know that boy was passing in front of his girlfriend's house three blocks away.

I didn't know whether that would work with my DeSoto or not, but I could try. So, sure enough, when I was still about two blocks from 619 Mountain View, I turned the key in the ignition and then turned it back right away; and that dear old car made a very satisfactory *bang.* I did it again, and again. Then I did it one more time as I was getting close to 619, killed the engine and let the DeSoto coast to a stop about three feet from the curb in front of Mrs. Linda Hollonbrook's house. It was a good thing there was no traffic on that street.

Then I pumped the gas pedal too many times before I turned on the ignition, and, sure enough, I had flooded the carburetor, so I was able to put on a good show of not being able to get the old thing started.

In case anybody was looking, I pouted a little and said, "Oh dear!" several times. I got out of the car and looked up the street and looked down the street and hesitated before I started tentatively up the walk.

It was a very decent house—not as big as the other Hollonbrook house or as stylish, but the man had given his divorced wife and his children a pleasant and adequate home—possibly the very same house in which they had all lived before the divorce. And if it was debt-free, it was more desirable than the house in which Alice Hollonbrook was living.

I heard the door chimes and waited less than a minute for the door to open.

It could be no other than Linda Hollonbrook, and I am afraid I understood why Holly had discarded her. She was in her early forties—naturally, she would be. She had been pretty once, probably in a healthy, unspoiled way—slightly pug nose, china blue eyes, otherwise-undistinguished features. If the face had been happy, she would still have been attractive. But the corners of her mouth sagged, suggesting a surly discontent. The Little Orphan Annie hairdo would have been wrong on anybody, but it had to be worst on her.

"Darling," I said—she was just a slip of a thing, no more than five foot two—"my old car seems to have broken down right here in front of your house. Would you be a real dear and let me use your phone?"

She nodded and opened the screen door.

"Oh, you are just an angel," I said, "allowing a complete stranger into your home this way. But gracious me, I must tell you my name. I am Ms. Hattie Gardner." That was my maiden name, but I didn't see any need to tell her I was the old lady in the *Famous DAR Murder Mystery*. Besides, lots of married women nowadays go around by their maiden name.

There was nothing else the woman could do but say, "I am Linda Hollonbrook."

" 'Beg pardon," I said, just as if I didn't know already.

She said it again, and I echoed, "Hollonbrook."

"Now if you'll just let me use your phone," I went on. And she led me to the hall, where the phone was on a little table. "Oh, and here is the directory," I said. I just kept my chatterbox going so she wouldn't have a chance to ask me a question I could not answer. I pretended to have trouble finding the number and turned one page several times, looking up and down both sides of it like a complete idiot. Then I called Maud's number the way I had planned. Maud picked up the phone on the second ring.

"Hello, is this Andy's?" I said quickly, so that there wouldn't be any chance that Maud would say something that Linda Hollonbrook would hear. It is so easy for another person to overhear a voice on the phone, and Linda was standing not four feet from me. I looked her in the eye with an innocent stare as much as to say, How could you possibly think I am anything other than a poor old stupid woman?

I told "Andy" my problem—the car just went *bang bang* several times, and then it stopped. Of course I paused now and then to give "Andy" time enough to ask me a question. But no, I assured him, the car hadn't made any funny noises other than the bangs. After a little bit of that, I put my hand over the mouthpiece and said to my blank-faced hostess, "Honey, Andy wants to know your address here."

She gave it to me, and of course I repeated it with the numbers in the wrong order so that she would have to correct me. By the time I had completed the call, I had her pretty well convinced that it was by accident that I had insinuated myself into her house.

"My dear, I am eighty-eight years old," I said, apropos of nothing. I saw she wasn't going to invite me to sit down. So I added, "And it is just so sweet of you to let me sit down here in your lovely home until Andy gets here to start my car." Then I plopped myself down in the most comfortable chair in her living room.

"Now don't you let me stop you from whatever you're doing. Just go right on. I'll be just fine here," I said, beaming with a beatific smile.

Of course the poor woman was not going off and leaving me, a complete stranger, alone for a minute. She sat down on the davenport, which was what I wanted her to do.

"I don't believe I caught your name," I said, taking my hankie out of my purse and patting the perspiration on my forehead and throat.

"Hollonbrook," she said.

"Do I know that name?" I said, applying the hankie to the back of my neck. "Seems to me I've heard it."

She looked as if she was taking a dose of Epsom salts as she replied, "You have probably heard of my former husband, the realtor, Charles Hollonbrook."

I looked surprised. "Oh, I suppose so." I paused just long enough so that it would seem that I was recollecting some little thing about Charles Hollonbrook—maybe the fact that he had another wife. "And darling, do you have children?" I went on.

"I have three."

"Oh, my dear, you must enjoy your children. Are they still young?"

She could hardly fail to talk about them after that—unless she had decided to be downright uncivil. Besides, women without husbands are that much more tied up in their children.

"My oldest, Jimmy, is nineteen. His sisters are eighteen and fifteen."

"I suppose the two oldest are in college."

"Linda Jean has just graduated from Stedbury High. I am thinking where I'll send her this fall, but I haven't made up my mind yet."

"Oh, my dear, you should reach a decision. Here it is June, and I believe there is often some difficulty with the colleges— can't get in and so on."

"Well," she admitted, "my former husband is recently deceased, and we are waiting for the estate to be worked out before we decide."

"Oh, yes," I seemed to remember, "your husband—former husband, that is—didn't he—didn't I read that he was killed?" You can bet I was watching her very closely in spite of the kindly look in my weak old eyes.

"He took his own life," she said.

I clicked my tongue in sympathy.

"He was not very good to the children," she broke out. "He wanted Linda Jean to go to the junior college at Estonia. He never seemed to care for any of the children—specially Jimmy. But there'll be plenty of money now. Jimmy has this chance to go to California and get into television."

Just then a girl in baby-doll pajamas came into the room. I glanced at my wristwatch. It was 11:20. The girl paid no attention to me. She had a regular haystack of dyed hair—had pimples. I couldn't help thinking that at her age I was at Catawba Hall, required to be up, dressed in school uniform, and have my bed made by 6:30. Then it was breakfast and chapel at 7:30. But Mama used to let me stay in bed until seven in the summer. It was a different world.

It turned out this was the youngest, Donna.

"Where are my jeans?" the girl demanded—and there was such a surly tone to her voice.

"They are in the dryer," her mother said. "I washed them this morning. You can probably take them out now."

The child flounced off to some other part of the house— utility room, I suppose.

"Your daughter is very attractive," I said.

Linda Hollonbrook actually smiled. "She is going to be a singer," she said. "Now that we are going to have money, I am going to see to it that my children have the things they should have had all along."

The smile had vanished, and in its place there was a look not of hate but perhaps something like victory. The poor woman was just consumed with the feeling that Charles Hollonbrook had wronged her.

"And is there much money?" I asked. It takes a good deal of nerve to get away with a question like that.

"Oh yes," she replied, apparently eager to talk about it.

"You know," she said, "Mr. Hollonbrook had the Ducky's restaurants in Maxwell and Eunice and here in Stedbury. And then there's Hollondale. Yes, Holly really knew how to make money; he just didn't want to give any of it to us. I had to beg him for the least thing. He made the biggest fuss over the children's teeth, and he was just stingy as can be about the girls' ballet lessons. And then when Jimmy was having so much trouble in high school—the teachers were so indifferent they wouldn't help him—his father refused to send him to military school. Jimmy would have been so handsome in uniform. Holly said Uncle Sam could be Jimmy's military school.

"And he could spend any amount on Alice," she continued. "But that's all changed now. They haven't found any will, and that means my children will get their share, after all. But it is going to be a while yet. They are still looking for a will. But they'll never find it."

Not find a will? She seemed very emphatic. Was it just specu-lation—a fantasy fulfillment of her dreams? Or did she know whereof she spoke? I didn't have time to wonder about that just then.

I heard a car come up and stop.

"That must be Andy," I said. Of course it wasn't—because there wasn't any Andy.

Then the screen door opened, and I heard, "Hey, there's an antique car out there!"

He was talking about my DeSoto. I guess it's something when you drive a car until it's an antique.

The young man was the noteworthy Jimmy. He was sallow—hollow-cheeked—stringy blond hair, none too clean-looking—hanging down in a ponytail halfway past his shoulders—earring in his ear—jeans, of course—torn so that there were just threads holding them together over his thighs—not tall—maybe five foot four or five.

Alice was short; Paula Stout was short; Linda was short; and here Jimmy Hollonbrook was short, too. Had Charles Hollonbrook been short? Was that part of his problem?

When I was a girl, I was very popular. Often was the time that I had five young men sitting at my feet on the porch at Catawba Hall. That's how I learned "the art of conversation." I talked, and I didn't talk about myself or other girls. I talked about the young men who were calling on me. And believe me, I complimented them highly—asked all about them—and thought it was just wonderful, whatever it was.

There's hardly anybody that doesn't need encouragement at some time or other. And it is so easy to give it to them. Why, I bet that Linda and Holly would still be married if she had just built up his self-esteem. You know we used to say, "Trains run on steam, but men run on self-esteem."

But that's getting away from the point, and it is an important one. Of all the boys that courted me, there wasn't one that was shorter than I was.

I don't know what it is about short men. They can be just as handsome, brainy, thoughtful, fine in every way, but I've noticed that a good many of them are sensitive about their height.

Well, I was tall, and that's not supposed to be a good thing for a woman. Yet it never crossed my mind to regret it.

But to get back to Charles Hollonbrook, it could be that being short had something to do with his drive and his insistence on excelling—specially in the sexual area.

So here was the son. I wondered what he would look like with his hair combed and cut—in a business suit—and without that earring in his ear.

"My, he's good-looking," I said in an aside to his mother. That surprised him.

"Come around here and let me get a look at you," I went on. "Your mother tells me you are interested in television. You must act in plays quite a lot."

"He's interested in production," his mother said. "He has a camcorder, and you should just see the excellent videotape he has made—he's just a natural at it."

"Your mother was telling me your father passed away recently," I said.

"Yeah." He said it rather awkwardly, but there was no regret in his voice. I wanted to ask him whether he had been with his dad much recently. But that would have been more than even I could get away with.

I felt I had learned all I could learn at that moment. The boy could easily have gotten hold of his father's gun and all that, and Paula Stout had said that Jimmy knew when his dad would be in Borderville. But could Jimmy work out a way to kill his dad in a locked room? Absolutely not.

I didn't have a very high opinion of the mother's brainpower. But it was no secret that she hated her former husband—no doubt spent her spare time thinking about it. There is no end to the meanness and old-fashioned spite a woman can scheme up if she keeps at it long enough.

And don't forget: The whole lot of the Mountain-View-Drive Hollonbrooks were ecstatic over the prospects of spending Holly's supposed wealth. I could believe that murder was not beyond the pale for that family—if they thought they could get away with it. Not at all beyond the pale, with that snarling mother wolf and her ravenous litter.

Since "Andy" would never come, it was time for me to engineer my graceful exit.

"Young man—" I said, then broke off. "What did you say your name was?"

"Jim."

"Young men are so good with equipment and machinery and things like that," I said, holding out my car keys. "Just take these and see if you can't get my car started so I can get away and leave your poor mother in peace."

And of course he did get it started, because there was nothing wrong with it except a flooded carburetor, and that had adjusted itself.

He was very interested in my car. Lots of interest in *it* and none in *me*, although I am an antique, too.

So I drove away. I don't know what they thought of me, but that doesn't matter.

KIMBERLIN MAYBURN

>> Harriet Bushrow <<

Maud had a nice lunch waiting for me when I got to the house. She has this lovely breakfast room that looks out to the garden of a neighbor across the street, and it's just as pleasant as can be.

We were sitting there with our iced tea. I had told Maud all about my visit with Linda Hollonbrook. She laughed and said, "Harriet, you are the beatingest thing I ever saw," which I could take in two ways: But I can tell you a thing or two about Maud. One time at Catawba Hall, she . . . but I had better not get into that.

Anyhow, Maud was having a good time being "on the fringe," as you might say, of my "investigations." And of course it was fun for her. It was her town, and little things would occur to her that I couldn't possibly have thought of. And one of those things was Kimberlin Mayburn. Maud was very interested in her.

"No," Maud agreed with me. "Kim Mayburn is not very likely as a suspect. But she was that man's mistress, and you can count on it that she knows more about his recent doings than Alice Hollonbrook does. You ought to talk to her."

"Maybe I should," I agreed. "Now tell me just who Kimberlin Mayburn is."

So Maud told me.

If any Yankee happens to read this, I'll have them to know that *who* a person is in the South has nothing to do with the present. It has to do with "past connections," which are very important. Connections don't have to be illustrious, but it's mighty bad if you don't have any. We don't know what to make of people who don't have connections. But as soon as we understand a person's connections, it's like fitting an important piece into a jigsaw puzzle. And society is a jigsaw puzzle, isn't it? Everybody has a place somewhere. He just needs to find it and "fit in."

Now to show how this works: Kimberlin Mayburn's father, who died in a car accident about ten years ago, was for a good many years a state senator from Stedbury's district. Being a state senator doesn't mean that a man is brilliant or honest or anything to brag about. But it puts him in a place. And leaving my own family out of it, Lamar's people were very distinguished. So here I am with just barely enough to scrape by on, but I have a place, and I am very secure in it, thank you.

So, when I got ready to call on Kimberlin Mayburn, all I had to do was call and say, "This is Mrs. L. Q. C. Lamar Bushrow"—and Kimberlin Mayburn would never be able to turn me down with a name like that.

But before I tell about my visit, I'll just state the facts Maud told me about Kimberlin Mayburn. First off, her mother was a Hartley from Raleigh, and the Hartleys were connected with the Millers and Longmeads of Georgia. (I had a cousin who married a Longmead.) Miss Kimberlin has been married twice—once to a naval officer from California, and the second time to a Frenchman with a taste for boys. So she is back in Stedbury using her maiden name again.

Now what kind of person would Kimberlin be? If there ever

was a case where a woman ought to call herself Ms. this was it.

She lives in a condominium. To my mind, that is a come-down, but then I belong to another age. They tell me condos are practical and convenient. And the kind of entertaining people do nowadays doesn't require a big house. So there she is in her condo. And the condo is in—you guessed it—Hollondale.

There are ten or twelve condos in that—I think they call it a complex. Anyhow, the apartments are built together, but they are separate and face in different ways, with lots of skylights and balconies and privacy walls and little dabs of lawn no bigger than a bed sheet. It's a real question whether you are ever going to find the right house number.

But I found it and rang the bell.

The door opened, to reveal a petite figure—there was that matter of height again—in a white silk blouse and a gray skirt. Violet eyes, blond hair, beautifully coiffured, and white jade earrings. This girl may have been around the track two times, but there had been thoroughbreds in the race.

Her voice was low in pitch, which I have always found attrac-tive. And she had no accent that I could identify. She invited me in very graciously to a high-ceilinged room with exposed beams.

The first thing I noticed was a Philadelphia reproduction Chippendale chair. There was a grand piano in the room also and a very good portrait of a woman in an evening dress like the ones we used to wear in the twenties.

"That's your grandmother," I said.

"Yes."

"She was a Longmead?"

"Yes."

"Georgia family?"

"Yes."

"My cousin Lida Jeffers married a Longmead from Chat-tahoochee County."

You see how it works. I had demonstrated that I knew where she belonged, and in doing so I had demonstrated where I belonged, although I have no notion in the world that Lida had married into the same family of Longmeads.

And Kimberlin Mayburn, for all her modern sophistication, had me pegged for an old lady very much like her grandma.

"I'm going to be very frank with you," I said after we were seated. "I know about you and Charles Hollonbrook, and I want you to know that I understand and offer you my sympathy."

A look of surprise came into her face and then changed into something that I didn't quite understand. I doubt whether she minded my knowing that she had been in a "relationship" with Charles Hollonbrook, but such a thing really ought not to be admitted publicly in a town like Stedbury. It wouldn't have been good for the district governor. And it must have been a well-kept secret, because Alice Hollonbrook hadn't known it was going on until they opened Chuck's bank box. No matter how liberated we may be nowadays, I doubt if an etiquette has been developed that decides whether the wife or the mistress stands by the casket in the funeral home during the viewing. Thus whatever feeling Kimberlin Mayburn may have had was a feeling that dared not speak its own name.

"How did you know?" Kim asked.

"It was the insurance policy," I said.

"He was going to leave Alice and marry me," Kim said—said it very simply.

I was cautious in accepting that at face value. Perhaps my doubt showed in my face.

"It would have happened if it hadn't been for this district governor thing."

Well, I could see that. There were duties connected with the office that were inconsistent with a process for divorce, a society wedding, a honeymoon, and all that goes with it. Besides, it was now apparent that he had not had the money for such as that—unless he had intended to use her money.

"And since that would put our marriage off for more than a year"—she was speaking rapidly, no doubt trying to convince herself—"Holly said that the insurance policy would be his pledge. He said . . ." The tears were now welling silently from eyes that once looked at Charles Hollonbrook with adoration.

"I mustn't talk like this," Kim told herself. She got up and took a tissue from a box on a writing table near the window. She blew her nose quietly, tossed the tissue into the wastebasket beside the table, and returned to her chair.

"It's the policy I came to talk to you about," I said, "because it looks to me like you are being cheated out of half a million dollars."

There is hardly anybody, no matter how wretched she feels, who isn't ready to talk about half a million dollars.

Kim looked at me in a blank way. "Dan Blake—that's the attorney for the estate—called and told me that the policy does not pay in the case of suicide."

"Exactly right," I said, "but can you tell me any reason why Charles Hollonbrook would want to kill himself?" Other than to get shut of those children, I might have added, but that would have been ugly.

"You and he were happy," I suggested. "He was district governor, beloved by Rotarians throughout the district, or at least they act that way. There may have been some little financial setbacks, but that wouldn't amount to anything for a man as energetic and resourceful as Mr. Hollonbrook. Now there hasn't been a close relation between him and his wife for several years, as I understand it. But in recent months, he seems to have found a deep and satisfying relationship with you. Surely you could tell me if there was any cause for suicide."

There was quite a little pause while Kim Mayburn looked me over in an anguished manner. She collected herself and said politely, although coolly, "Would you please tell me just where you come into this."

"I am merely interested in seeing that justice is done," I said.

"Well, you are right," she said. "Holly had business problems. He mentioned them to me. But he was absolutely confident. He was the strongest man I have ever known . . . and yet he needed something. I know what they said about him—that he was a stud, but to me he was very tender. He had been disappointed in that first marriage—and as for Alice, she was as cold and hard as a stone. I was ready to give him what he needed and no one had ever given."

I suppose she thought that was all true. But frankly, I thought that would have been a waste of generosity—which, of course, was neither here nor there.

"So you know of no motive for his suicide," I said. "Now think real hard. Is there someone who might have wanted Charles Hollonbrook out of the way or somebody who might have hated him?"

Frowning, Kim studied the carpet. After a minute, she said, "I don't know of anybody who hated *him*, but I'm pretty sure there was one who hated *me*."

That didn't seem to be what I was looking for. But I asked who it was.

"It's that woman in his office."

That honey-sweet doer of golden deeds? That perfect keeper of the office who was so helpful to Alice Hollonbrook? And what could Paula Stout have done to cause Kimberlin Mayburn to speak with such venom?

Kim saw the surprise on my face. "Oh yes, she does," she said. "That insipid little judgmental hypocrite has hated me from the beginning. She with her little snub nose in the air! What right has she to be so pious?" I could hardly believe what I saw in Kim's face—anger, hatred, a mishmash of every ugly feeling you would care to think of.

I began to wonder about the girl who sat before me. She had seemed so self-possessed one moment, and the next moment was ready to fly off the handle before I could say Jack Robinson.

"Now, darling, just be calm and tell Mrs. B. all about it."

Maybe it was the slangy way I referred to myself as Mrs. B. that surprised the child. Whatever it was, her mood modified somewhat, and she began.

"It started soon after I took this condominium. I had been through so much, and now I was at home again among my own people, although the people here are not my own people—really. They don't accept me. My life has been so different, and they can't understand someone like me.

"After all I had been through, I needed rest. And this condo was just big enough for me to have my most precious things. But then this and that went wrong." She paused and looked sadly into depths of vacancy.

"What went wrong?" I asked.

"The water heater."

"The water heater?" Now a water heater can be aggravating, as I well know; but that a hot-water heater could be more than a mere irritation made me wonder if the girl was sane.

"Yes, the water heater. In the shower, sometimes the water would run cold as ice and then suddenly it was scalding. Then when I would adjust the handle, it would happen again. I called the office the very first time that happened, and Miss Stout said she would send the plumber right away. But she did not. The plumber did not come for four whole days, although I called the office every day and informed little Miss Stout of the matter in a firm but polite way.

"On the fourth day, Holly came and tested the hot water. That was the first time that . . ."

I don't know what happened that "first time." The poor girl's voice had just died on her.

"There, there, dear," I said soothingly. I think I got the picture. This sprout from an aristocratic family had made a pest of herself about little things that went wrong in her condominium. If it hadn't been the hot water, it would have been the garage door or the light switch in the kitchen. And her constant complaints were enough to rile a saint—Paula Stout, that is.

And I dare say that this young woman before me, when she wanted to summon her lover, had to call him at the office, for she certainly couldn't call him at the house. That kind of thing can interfere with office routine. I could imagine that Paula Stout would get just as irritated by Kim Mayburn's incessant calls as Kim was irritated by her hot-water heater.

Then, too, I could see it from Holly's point of view. All I had to do was look around that room. There was good taste everywhere—and family items—not the decorator-bought stuff that Alice had. As for Kim herself, no matter what else she might be, she was exquisite. All in all, I would say there was a trap here for a man like Charles Hollonbrook.

"Oh, how I do understand!" I said, although I am afraid there was a little double interpretation that could have been placed on my words.

"That is kind of you," she said. Her voice was calm. She was once again the poised and gracious person who had opened the door when I rang. "These days, you know, are lonely," she said. "I sit here with my thoughts. I am all right. I tell myself I am all right."

"I'm sure you are, my dear," I said. I hoped it sounded encouraging.

Then she said, "He used to call me every day when he was out of town. We would talk—oh, on and on. And now that is over." The tears were definitely on their way.

Oh Lord, I thought, this is more than I want to hear about! So I wound up the visit and talked right much so she didn't have a chance to go off the rails.

After that experience, I was glad to get back to Maud's house.

THE WOMEN

>>*Maud Tinker Bradfield*<<

I can't remember when I have had such a good time as I have had with Harriet here—not since before Mr. Bradfield died, anyhow. It is amazing. Hattie and I can go ten years without seeing each other, and then it is just as if the years have not passed at all. It seems that the rest of the world has changed, but we are the same.

There's still arthritis, you know, and we begin to talk about an old friend, and neither of us can remember the name. Then I look at Hat, and she looks at me, and we both giggle like schoolgirls.

And this visit has been so exciting for me. Since it is hard for me to get out as much as I used to, I sit at home too much and watch whodunits on the television. Lo and behold, Harriet comes along and brings a real whodunit right into my living room.

So, whenever she came back from one of her ventures and interviews and so on, I fixed us tall glasses of iced tea or cups of good hot coffee, and she had to tell me all about it.

Well! When Harriet got back from her visit to Kimberlin Mayburn, the first thing she said was, "What in the world is wrong with that woman?"

"Oh," I said, "didn't I tell you?" I don't know how I failed to do it. I guess it was because the French husband was attracted to young boys—you know nice girls didn't know about such things when I was young—and so there were some things we didn't understand and didn't care to know about.

Nowadays, everybody talks about homosexuality, and it's only old women like us that think anything about it.

So it must have been that I got wrapped up in that part of the story and didn't mention that Kim had had a complete nervous breakdown. I think she had had one before—when her marriage to that naval officer broke up.

Whether that was true or not, after she said good-bye to the Frenchman, she must have had a *real* breakdown, because they had her in a private sanitarium over there for a while.

Of course, you never know about those things. It's rather stylish to have a mental problem. And the Mayburns were always stylish. And from all reports, Kimberlin was supposed to be all right.

But the poor girl! Only think of it! A romance developing out of a faulty hot-water heater—and the Mayburns always considered a leading family! Well, what has this world come to?

I don't know a thing about psychology, but it sounded to me like the girl was somewhat cracked, and maybe the Frenchman wasn't any more offbeat than she was.

We talked about that for quite a while, and then I said, "Isn't it amazing the number of women that come into this? Just look: There's that first wife. Ever since the divorce, she has complained about how stingy he was with her, until half the town won't listen to her anymore. And when her darling boy asks his father for money to go off on some wild-goose chase and the father refuses, she is just sure the boy's chances in life have ended. But with Charles Hollonbrook dead, she thinks her children are going to inherit a small fortune. You never know what the lioness will do for her cubs."

"And if you just bring the boy into it," Harriet observed, "you have a combination there that could pull it off. There is knowledge of Hollonbrook's whereabouts and possible accessibility to the weapon."

"But," I insisted, "it would be the mother who would have to plan it, don't you think?"

Harriet looked skeptical. She wasn't impressed with the brains of either the mother or the son.

And then, of course, there was Alice Hollonbrook. If you believed what she had told Harriet, her husband's death left her practically destitute. But then she might not have known about that beforehand. And there is the other man. She says he won't marry her, but that's what she says *now*. What did she think *then*? And suppose she had not known that the other man would not marry her and had found out that Hollonbrook was about to divorce her. She has no children and would not have gotten any child support out of the divorce. And that insurance policy would go by the board when Hollonbrook stopped payment of premiums.

We discussed this quite some while. Surely Alice Hollonbrook had known where her husband would be each night he would be gone, probably knew which motel, in fact. And who had better access to the gun? She did not have a real alibi. The one thing that said she was not the culprit was the fact that the death looked like suicide. If she was the murderer, surely she would not have contrived to lose $500,000 through a faked suicide. But then perhaps she had not known that the policy would not pay off in a case of that sort.

Then there was another person to consider. Paula Stout obviously knew where Hollonbrook would be each night he was away, because she had no doubt made the arrangements herself. And she was feeding the dog. So she could get into the house and get the key to the gun drawers in the basement.

Could she have been still another of Hollonbrook's lights of love? Considering the physical attractions of his certified mistresses—first Alice, then Desiree, and finally Kim—Harriet and I had to strain our imaginations to conceive the possibility. But at the very least she could have an old-fashioned crush on Charles Hollonbrook; and unrequited love, though out of style, can cause people to do violent things.

And Paula was in a better position than Alice to know of the progress of Hollonbrook's affair with Kim Mayburn. Perhaps Paula and Alice had been in confidence in the matter.

But Desiree, the golf pro's wife, could have been a factor. We talked about that for a while. She was ancient history; and then there was the inescapable fact that her husband was down in Florida—too far off to get wind of Charles Hollonbrook's doings. How could Bucky Patterson get hold of the pistol and the silencer? But there might be unseen gears and wheels at work here. Still, we would have to close the book on Bucky and Desiree unless something new turned up that we didn't yet know.

Five women! I don't know why it took the feminists so long to discover that it is women who cause things to happen.

"There is one more woman," Harriet announced suddenly.

I counted them again and still got five. Linda, Alice, Desiree, Paula, and Kimberlin Mayburn.

"Maybe six or seven," Harriet said. "Have you forgotten Kitty Herbert and Caroline Rawlings?"

For the moment, I couldn't think who they were.

"The woman whose picture was in the clipping Alice Hollonbrook found in the bank box," Harriet prompted. "She could be one, or she could be two women. Anyhow, we have two more names.

"And we don't know a thing about either name," she added. Then she said, "I have a hunch."

>> *Harriet Bushrow* <<

Now didn't Maud write that up nicely! And she left it so I could pick it up just at the right point.

Estonia Savings and Loan—in Estonia, North Carolina—and Estonia only forty-five miles from Stedbury. It would take almost an hour for me to get there, an hour to do my business, and almost an hour to get back.

I left Maud's house at 9:45 the morning after our foregoing conversation, telling her to expect me back certainly before one. Since I had no idea what I could expect in Estonia, I would just have to feel my way.

Now some of my readers may never have heard of Stedbury, North Carolina. But the town I am calling Estonia (not its real name) is quite a different matter. The sign at the city limit says the population is 63,000, and of course the mills they have there are famous. Being so much larger than Stedbury, Estonia is where people from Stedbury go to shop at stores with a larger selection of merchandise.

So even though it's a mill town, Estonia has amenities, I suppose you would call them—a big, modern hospital—very impressive—several nice-looking motels that I passed on my way into town—and other indications of prosperity.

Where there are mills, there is bound to be some money; and while money doesn't necessarily mean nice people, I've noticed that "nice" people generally gather where the money is—bankers, lawyers, doctors, educators. . . . Estonia has two colleges, you know—and all those people have wives, and the wives belong to civic clubs, social clubs, and study clubs. Of course, it's not what you would call an "old" community—not that kind of place at all. It wouldn't take four generations before a person could "belong" there. A hundred years ago, Estonia wasn't much more than a whistle-stop. But now I'm sure it thinks of itself as a very special place indeed.

When I stopped at a gas station, the attendants all came running. At home, nobody ever notices my old DeSoto because they are accustomed to seeing me in it. But when on very rare occasions I go out of town, it draws lots of attention. You would think I was a queen the way those young men want to look under the hood, clean the windshield, and even run a chamois over the chrome.

So I took advantage of all that interest to get directions for reaching the Estonia Savings and Loan.

"Not hard to find," the young man said. He told me to go straight a certain distance, then turn left a certain distance and count the signal lights, and I don't remember what all. But when I got him to slow down, I understood enough of what he said to get there without feeling completely lost more than twice.

Estonia Savings and Loan is not in the heart of the city, but on a commercial street with places where they sell and install car mufflers, deal in wholesale candy, run weight-loss centers, and things like that. Most of the buildings have been there awhile. But some of the places look as if they were put up not very long ago.

Estonia Savings and Loan is one of the new places. It's very "architectural"—trying to look colonial. But the windows are too big and the brick is too pink. There is a nice parking area and everything around the building is landscaped. You could tell by its looks that the Estonia Savings and Loan was up-to-the-minute. Yes, and later on I learned that, like some other savings and loan companies that were up-to-the-minute, it was in trouble.

I parked and entered the building, to find myself in a large area. To the left was a reception desk. Directly in front of me was a wall paneled in walnut that had a few photographs hanging on it, and to the sides there were chromium chairs pretending to be upholstered in leather.

"Can I help you?" the young lady at the desk asked.

I said, "Yes, I am Mrs. L. Q. C. Lamar Bushrow." That name will get me into anyplace I would care to go. But just to make sure I would get the attention I wanted, I added a little something, saying, "I am the aunt of Mr. Charles Hollonbrook of Hollonbrook Realty in Stedbury. No doubt you may be aware that my nephew passed away a little over a month ago."

This information seemed to make a further impression. "I am here about the estate."

Estate has such a wonderful ring to it! The young woman looked at me again, and this time she really saw me.

I said, "I am here to discuss my late nephew's indebtedness to your company."

Now what would *you* make of an eighty-eight-year-old woman in hat and gloves claiming to be an heir to an estate that was in debt to Estonia Savings and Loan? You would make just what the young woman did. She decided to hand the problem over to somebody else.

"How do you spell that name?" she asked.

"Mrs. L. Q. C. Lamar—L-A-M-A-R—Bushrow—B-U-S-H-R-O-W," I said very deliberately. She wrote it down.

"If you'll just take a seat," she said, "I'll find out if Mr. Stockard can see you." Then, although there was one of those intercom things on her desk, she went off into the back of the building because, obviously, there was something that she wanted to tell Mr. Stockard and didn't want me to hear.

I sat down in one of the chairs, where I could hardly help examining the walnut-paneled wall—probably not real walnut at all, but it made a statement. And the photographs on the wall made a statement, too.

The photo immediately in front of me showed a man of about forty with an earnest expression. A small placard under the picture read, VINCENT T. LARSON, SEC. TREAS. Next to that picture was another, of a man in his fifties. KENNETH GIBBERT, VICE. PRES. And there was a third one: BEN H. RAWLINGS, PRES.

So, you see, I was on the right track.

Just then, the young receptionist came around the corner with Mr. Stockard. In a conspiratorial way, she pointed him toward me. He approached with constrained curiosity in his face.

"Mr. Stockard," I said, "I think I had better see Mr. Rawlings."

"I'm sure," he replied, and looked at the slip of paper that he held in his hand, "Mrs. Bushrow—yes—I am sure I can help you."

"No, I don't think you can," I said. "Mr. Rawlings is the man I want to see."

"Mr. Rawlings is in conference," he objected.

"Very well," I said. "Tell him I'll see him as soon as he is out of conference," and I folded my hands over my purse and sat there like Buddha.

The young people looked at each other. Mr. Stockard said something that I did not catch to the receptionist, and the two of them went back into the hind parts of the building.

Pretty soon, the gentleman who matched the photograph of Rawlings came out, followed by the receptionist and Stockard.

I rose and gave Rawlings my hand.

"Good morning," I said. "It is so good of you in your busy schedule to see me. I am here to clear up a matter that is a mystery to me but may be of some importance to you." I gave him my knowingest look, and he got the message.

"If you will please step back here into my office," he said, indicating the general area from which he had come.

The minute I stepped into the office, I knew I had been right. There on the windowsill stood a picture of a woman who could easily be the same person whose picture appeared in the clipping Alice Hollonbrook and her lawyer had found in the Hollonbrook bank box.

"Is that your wife?" I asked.

He nodded.

"She looks very sweet," I observed. "Do you have children?"

He nodded again.

"Is this also a picture of your wife?" I asked, taking the clipping out of my purse and handing it to him.

The poor man sat down and leaned over his desk, his head in his hands.

"Why can't you people leave us alone?" he moaned.

"Then I take it that Charles Hollonbrook knew of your wife's identity and used that fact to blackmail you."

He looked at me, wondering what would come next. "Something like that," he said.

"Please let me disabuse your mind of the misapprehension for which I am responsible," I said. "I am not the aunt of Mr. Charles Hollonbrook and am in no way connected with him, though in a sense I represent Alice Hollonbrook, the widow. She is not aware of the significance of this clipping, and neither she nor I have any intention of revealing Mrs. Rawlings's secret."

His attitude became one of relief immediately. Suddenly realizing that I had remained standing, he rectified his omission of courtesy by placing a chair for me and urging me to be seated.

After he had got that matter straightened out, he asked me just how I was involved. I explained that many people had begun to think Charles Hollonbrook had been murdered and that I was helping Mrs. Hollonbrook as she tried to get to the bottom of the question. And that was true.

Mr. Rawlings said he harbored no hard feelings against Mrs. Hollonbrook and could understand that she would want to clear up any mystery connected with her husband's death, but he did not see what that had to do with him.

"I might as well tell you the truth," I said. "That poor girl— Alice Hollonbrook—will be up against it when you foreclose on those notes unless we can prove that her husband did not die by his own hand. But you needn't worry. She has no idea of continuing the blackmail. If you can give me a firm alibi for the night of May 26, I will give you the clipping and guarantee that you will have no further concern in that quarter."

And then he told me all about it. Rawlings's wife was a Miss Cameron from Hainsford. She married a man named Herbert, who was a sadist and tortured her unmercifully, until one night she stabbed him. Because she could not prove that on that occasion her life was in danger, she was found guilty and sentenced to twenty years, but she was pardoned five years later. Two years after that, she became Mrs. Rawlings and doubly concealed her identity by adopting the given name Caroline.

The Rawlings had come to Estonia, where Mr. Rawlings prospered with the Estonia Savings and Loan. The couple were popular, and Mrs. Rawlings became prominent in the social life of the town. She was on the board of the Salvation Army, had been an officer in service organizations, and had made for herself a very satisfactory life.

The poor man! What he must have felt when Charles Hollonbrook appeared! Having grown up in Hainsford, Hollonbrook recognized Caroline Rawlings as Kitty Herbert. The earliest loans Hollonbrook had received from Estonia Savings and Loan had been legitimate enough. But when Rawlings denied later loans, Hollonbrook had hinted expertly that his "friendship" in the direction of Ben and Kitty Herbert Rawlings was a "two-way street."

Caroline Rawlings was at that time running for election to the school board. If it had got abroad that she had been in the penitentiary, she would have been defeated, and the knowledge that Caroline had killed her first husband, no matter how extenuating the circumstances, would have shaken all her social contacts. That was something Rawlings could not face. In view of the coming election, he had made the loan against his better judgment, supposing that would be the end of it. But it wasn't the end. Each new loan was going to be the end, and each new loan was only slightly more risky than the last, until the investment in Hollondale Estates had become a troublesome burden to Estonia Savings and Loan.

"We are not ready just yet to close our doors, Mrs.—" again he looked at my name on the slip of paper the receptionist had given him. "Mrs. Bushrow," he continued, "but we are in straits, and the Hollonbrook loans are a tremendous liability to us. If it had not been for—well, for that scrap of paper you found among Hollonbrook's securities—we would never have made the later loans. And if we had made them, we would have foreclosed.

"But in view of Mrs. Hollonbrook's generosity as to the— well, that scrap of paper—we will put off the foreclosure as long as possible.

"As for where we were on the night of May 26—Mrs. Rawlings and I were soundly sleeping after a very exciting and rewarding but also tiring day. May 26 was the date on which our son was married to Miss Angie Nugent."

Well, that did indeed seem to remove the Rawlings family from suspicion. Very few parents could occupy their minds with murder—a murder as elaborate as that of Charles Hollonbrook—and the wedding of a son at the same time. Besides, I could hardly expect the man to have an impartial witness with him in the middle of the night, which, after all, was when the crime took place.

Aside from the alibi, there would be the question of the gun and how it was obtained, and I did not see how Rawlings could have gotten hold of that pistol and silencer from a locked drawer in a locked house with which he was not familiar and in a city at some distance from Estonia.

"Your explanation is fair enough," I said. I handed the paper to Mr. Rawlings. He took it, placed it in a large ashtray on his desk, and lit a match to it.

As the flames licked up and the paper shriveled into a fragile ash, it occurred to me to ask, "And where did your son's marriage take place?"

"In Boone."

I wondered if I had done the right thing to surrender that clipping. Boone, North Carolina, you see, is just a skip and a jump across the mountains from Borderville.

THE SUICIDE NOTE

>> *Maud Tinker Bradfield* <<

Harriet is right when she says that old women make good detectives. We sit alone in the house, and if we have enough sense not to be able to stand TV all day, we just have a few things to think about. So we think about them and think about them until we get them sorted out.

When Harriet went off to Estonia, I was alone in the house, and in the quiet I began to review what we had been talking about the day before.

Whoever killed Charles Hollonbrook had to have had a motive and some way of getting hold of that gun. That's all well and good. But there is something else.

There had been a note found by the body—a note that looked like a suicide note. But Harriet didn't think the contents of the note were quite the thing for a suicide.

All right then. If the note was written on Charles Hollonbrook's personalized notepad, the fellow who killed Hollonbrook must have gotten one of those notes from Hollonbrook himself. So when Harriet got back from Estonia, I put it to her. I said, "Hat, you said the note that was left by the body came from Charles Hollonbrook's personalized notepad. Don't you think we ought to look into that? We need to find out how the murderer got hold of that note."

She said, "That's right."

"Well, don't you think we ought to get that worked out?"

"Yes indeed," she said.

"And while there are probably a certain number of people who could have gotten the gun and a certain number who could have gotten the note, if they are not all the same people, wouldn't that cut down the number of people who could have done it?" I reasoned.

It was worth looking into, and we talked about it for a while. Harriet said, "I wonder if that man had more than one pad."

"Easy enough to find out," I said. "I'll call Paula Stout and ask her."

I never was what you would call a friend of Paula's or of her mother, who died six or eight years ago. But I can remember when I used to buy Girl Scout cookies from Paula, so it was less awkward for me to call her than for Harriet to do it.

Paula reported that there had been six pads originally. One pad had been placed in the pad holder on his desk. He had taken one pad home. And another had been placed on his desk when the first pad ran out. There were three pads left in the supply cupboard.

That didn't seem to get us very far, because the sheet from the notepad wouldn't have done the murderer any good if Charles Hollonbrook hadn't written on it. So the murderer had to be the one who had originally received the note or someone who had had access to the note after it was laid aside.

"Now tell me exactly what was in the note," I said.

Harriet got her purse and took out the little notebook she jots everything down in. She leafed through a few pages and found the place. She handed me the notebook and I read: "Sorry to disappoint you, but I can't make it today. C.J.H."

"That *is* odd," I mused. "I mean as a suicide note. Who was supposed to read it? The Rotarians? That doesn't sound like a

note you would write to a Rotary Club to tell them—well—" I
broke off.

"To say to them that you would rather die than eat their meat
loaf and English peas?" Harriet concluded the sentence for me.

Actually, I would think a suicide note would be rather daunt-
ing. If I had to write one, I think, in preference I would give up
the idea of killing myself. Good heavens! Suppose you didn't
spell everything right!

However that may be, I felt sure that Charles Hollonbrook
would have thought up something a good deal more impressive
than the note that was found by his body.

"I can't make it *today.*" Now that word *today*—that's what
you say when you wake up in the morning. And you say *today*
at night when you look back over the past day. But even after
midnight, you don't speak of the coming day as *today.* You call
it *tomorrow.* And the way I understood it, Hollonbrook had
died at night.

I said all this to Harriet, and all she would comment was, "I've
already told you; it is not a suicide note."

"But what kind of person would he write a note like that to?"
I asked. " 'Sorry to disappoint you—' It sounds like he is breaking an appointment, probably lunch or a meeting someone else
has made plans for, or maybe he failed to do something for
someone—and he just pushes it aside. He surely couldn't write
a note like that to someone he cared about."

"Why not?" Harriet wanted to know. "He could slip it into a
box of chocolates and send it to her. Or do men still send
chocolates to the 'other woman'?"

"I wouldn't know," I answered. "But I see what you mean.
The note could be just a kind of explanation for the gift. If we
look at it that way, there could be any number of those notes
in existence."

"It strikes me more like a note to somebody he doesn't have
to be polite to," Harriet said, "somebody who takes orders,

somebody who expects to be at his disposal. The best bet for that would be the girl in his office."

"Or his wife," I said, just to be cute.

"No," Harriet said, "that note wasn't written to his wife—and it wasn't written to his ex-wife, either. It has been some time since either one of those ladies would be what you would call disappointed if Charles Hollonbrook did not show up."

We both sat quietly for a minute or so—it was like those times when you are working a crossword puzzle and can't think of a word.

Then Harriet said, "Maud, you are right. He wrote that note to some one or some people he didn't have to be polite to— that means people who won't take offense because they know him so well or because the circumstances don't matter to them. Why couldn't that note be intended for his gun club?

"I've got their names right here." She leafed through the pages of her notebook. "Here they are: Pete Gambrill, Don Kelsey, J. D. Robinson, and Mark Fuller. Do you know any of them?"

Well, I didn't know the Kelseys or the Fullers. But I knew J. D. Robinson by sight. He has a sign-painting shop on Second Street, and Jay—my husband, now deceased, knew him in the Shrine. And Pete Gambrill is somebody I can't live without. He is a heating and air-conditioning engineer. He looked after the furnace at our home on Fifth Street, where Jay and I lived for forty years. He kept that old furnace going long after they stopped making replacement parts. And now that I have this little place, he takes care of my heat pump.

Harriet was right much taken with her idea about the gun club, and I saw that she wanted to follow it up, so I went to the phone.

Pete was in the office and wasn't busy. I said, "You are going to have a visit from two decrepit old women who want your advice."

Pete said, "Wheel them in." That was just like him.

I would guess Pete would be about fifty. He is a little on the heavyset side—has a bald spot on the crown of his head. I thought he and Harriet ought to get along pretty well.

When we came into his office—it was a horrible mess—he jumped up and said, "Mrs. Bradfield, you told me a fib. You said two *old* ladies were going to come to see me."

But he didn't get a rise out of *me*. I've known him too long. I introduced Harriet, and it turned out that he had already heard about her because his daughter has a part-time job in the library. He hurriedly cleaned off the only other chair in the office.

"But where will you sit?" I asked.

"Oh, I'll just sit here on the corner of the desk," he said, pushing the telephone and a pile of papers off a spot hardly big enough to accommodate him. He half-leaned and half-sat there—an oversized, round-faced cherub beaming at us.

Harriet explained what she wanted to know and why she wanted to know it.

He said he could tell us about it.

It seems that the gun club didn't have any very formal organization, but they generally got together on Saturday mornings about 10:30 or 10:45 to practice on the range in the basement of the Hollonbrook house.

Since the members had their own keys, they could get into the basement when neither of the Hollonbrooks was at home. If Holly was at home when any of the club members came in and began to shoot, he would come down and join in the shooting.

But if he wasn't going to be at home, he would place a note in the crevice between the glass and the frame of the door to his rifle cabinet. And the note was always the same. "Sorry to disappoint you, but I can't make it today."

"Now, Mrs. Bushrow," Pete said, "and with apologies to you, Mrs. Bradfield, if you have found out anything about Holly, you know he was a ladies' man. And those notes meant that where he was—was with one of his ladies.

"You see, Mrs. Hollonbrook plays golf, and she was in the habit of playing with her foursome at the country club. And afterward, she would have lunch with the other ladies.

"Those notes got to be a real joke, because"—Pete paused and looked mischievous—"because he *was making* it."

"Shame on you," I said.

But of course it was perfectly true. And the explanation made sense. Harriet thanked Pete and said that he had been a great help.

"Maud," she said as we were driving home, "we know now at least one way that the murderer could have gotten the note.

"Hollonbrook might find out at breakfast that his wife would be gone from the house from about ten o'clock in the morning until maybe one-thirty in the afternoon. Then he could call his sweetie pie on the telephone to let her know he would be with her soon. He could write his note—always the same. And probably he knew what his buddies understood from *make it.* It had the further advantage of being a way of publicizing his conquest, you see.

"Then he would come home before Alice did, take down the note, and maybe open the drawer to get his pistol out for some target practice. So he could have dropped the note into the drawer, and Alice would never have found it.

"But if all of this is true," she concluded, "we are right back where we were, because any of the others who had access to the pistol could have found the note in the same place."

MY VISIT TO VIC DOUGLASS

>> Harriet Bushrow <<

I woke up the next morning trying to think what it was I had had in the back of my mind to do. There were so many threads leading this way and that way, and they all seemed to be balled up in a big mess. The name of Douglass came to mind. I had written it down in my memorandum book, but somehow I kept ignoring it.

Hollonbrook and Douglass was the name of the firm when Charles Hollonbrook first came to town. And I had already concluded that some kind of spat had developed that had busted up the combination. Although that had been a long time ago, perhaps it would be good to find out about it. So I put the question to Maud: Did she know this Vic Douglass?

He was a very nice man, she said, with a modest little wife and two daughters. Disciples, she said. His name was Vic and his wife was Nancy—just a plain, nice couple.

With that kind of recommendation, I thought, Thank the Lord I'm not going to run into anything exotic like people who go off on yachts with gentlemen friends from Baltimore or crazy people who had to divorce their French husbands. People like that are interesting, but enough is enough.

So I followed Maud's directions about how to get to his office, and I didn't have any trouble at all.

It was just a tiny little building—one room for the office and, I suppose, a washroom at the back. The furniture was plain and old—just practical, you know—no upholstery—just plain wood chairs. There were venetians on the windows but no drapes—linoleum tiles on the floor—no carpeting.

Vic Douglass was a heavyset gentleman in his late forties. He had a pleasant, open face and black hair. Without being what you would call handsome, he was good-looking.

He said, "Good morning, ma'am. How can I help you?"

I told him who I was and why I wanted to talk to him.

"So you think old Holly was murdered?" he said. He wasn't exactly smiling, but the idea didn't seem to bother him.

"Whether he killed himself," he went on, "or somebody finally got him, I would say Charles Hollonbrook had been on a collision course as long as I have known him."

The story began when Vic and Holly were at Granville State College. Vic's fraternity was in trouble with the dean on account of grades. But Vic had a certain freshman for his lab partner in his chemistry class, and the freshman—that was Hollonbrook, of course—was just a crackerjack student, making A's and all that.

The upshot was that Holly was taken into the fraternity to raise their grades.

Holly's people weren't what you would call well-off and Hainsford is just a very rural small town. So being at Granville State and being in a fraternity, Holly was in a different world from the one he had known. What did he do then but take Vic as a kind of model.

We see that so often, you know, with a young person who is not sure of himself. That is why it is so important to have a sense of family. I could never in this world have forgotten that I was a Gardner and that my mother was a Hadley.

Anyhow, Holly attached himself to Vic, who was two years

ahead of him in college. Vic graduated, got married, and went to work for his father. And Holly graduated, too, but he got drafted and went to the Vietnam War.

In the army, he was just the way he had been in college. He got to be a first lieutenant and was cited for bravery and got several medals. Then he was badly wounded and given a medical discharge.

He came back home to Linda, the girl he had married just before he went to Vietnam. In the meantime, Vic's father had died, and Vic had come into a little money.

The two friends got together and opened their realty firm in Stedbury, which looked like it had a future then.

Just as I had noticed from looking at all those years of the Stedbury *Gazette,* Douglass and Hollonbrook had had all the business they could handle. Vic was frank to admit that Holly was the best salesman he had ever seen. His experience in the war had given him a kind of assurance. And with the medals and the good looks, there was a kind of glamour about him. But it was just his constant drive that put him ahead in whatever he did.

"I don't think he was smarter than anybody else," Vic said. "He just didn't hesitate to do whatever would get him what he wanted."

And that brought the story down to the episode of Featherstone Plastics.

Everyone has heard of Featherstone Plastics. I dare say there is not a house in the country that doesn't have at least fifteen items made by Featherstone.

Well, Vic heard that Featherstone was thinking of opening several plants in the South. And there was a piece of farmed-out land that could be gotten for very little. So the firm took out a loan and bought the property.

Meanwhile, the chamber of commerce was working tooth and nail to bring the Featherstone plant to Stedbury and it looked like Featherstone would take the property that Hollonbrook and Douglass had to offer.

Then behind Vic's back, Holly found another site. The owner had just died, and the heirs were eager to sell the property and divide the proceeds.

Holly, on his own, without saying a word to Vic, scraped up every penny he had and took an option on the property; in ten days' time, he sold it to Featherstone.

That broke up the firm. Poor Vic was left with the other property, which then had no value. All of Vic's money was tied up in that land, with no prospect of getting it back.

"Mrs. Bushrow," he said, "if Holly had been killed fifteen years ago, I would have been your prime suspect. It wasn't just what he had done to me. He did it to my family, too. I tell you, we went through some pretty hard times."

"And you don't feel the same way now?" I asked.

"No, not really," he replied. "It's too sad a story. Holly had a potential and he used it. Everything fell before him. But what a price he paid!"

In spite of all the dirt I know about Charles Hollonbrook, I had a feeling for what Vic Douglass was saying. All the same, there were other things that I wanted to know.

"Was he always after the women, the way they say he was?" I asked.

Vic got a faraway look in his eyes. "No," he said, "when I first knew him, he was making too many A's to chase girls. The brothers in the fraternity, even though they wanted his grades, ragged him hard about being out of it as far as the sex scene went. I wouldn't guarantee what happened after I left Granville. Linda Logan, the first wife, was a pretty little thing—sweet—small-town background—not all that bright. He may have been to bed with her by the time they graduated. But he married her. That used to be done—not at Berkeley perhaps. But at Granville State College, the girls still expected it."

He was silent for a moment. He was thinking back to that earlier day, as we all do.

"Linda wasn't meant for a man like Holly. She tried, but she didn't have it. Before the children came, she did her best to keep up. She would go to parties and drink along with the others, but she would just get tiddly, and people would say, 'Poor Holly, why did he ever marry that woman?'

"But then Alice—you know she was in his office. She was a small-town girl, too. I think they began sleeping together about a year after she came to work for him.

"The delay," he added dryly, "was occasioned by an affair that had started before Alice came into the picture.

"I suppose you've seen Alice. She's very cool these days—good-looking—clotheshorse. From an outside point of view, she is the ideal Mrs. Charles Hollonbrook. Holly couldn't stay away from other women."

Vic looked at me a second or two with a glint in his eye. "I know what you want to ask me," he said. "You want to know if it ever happened with my wife. The answer is no—not that he wouldn't have tried if he thought he could. My wife is as true as a plumb line. As a judge of character, I have made one major mistake. That was Holly Hollonbrook. But I picked the right woman, and in my marriage I am the happiest man in town. That's why I don't hold anything against Holly anymore. He could never have had what I've got."

I thanked Vic. He got up when I did. I couldn't help saying, "I believe from the way you talk you are from Georgia."

"Yes, I am."

"And you know who the Bushrows are."

"Of course I do."

Now wasn't that nice?

LUNCH WITH HARRIET
AT THE CLUB

>> Maud Tinker Bradfield <<

At our age, no matter how much zip and zing you still have, there is just a certain amount you can do. With Harriet working so hard to clear up that mystery, I was afraid she would wear herself out.

My daughter, Tink, lives here with her husband and the two youngest children, Bob and Ruth. Tink and Jeff had three children pretty much in a row. And then it was a long time before Tink had the twins when she was forty. They are seventeen years old now, and just as normal for that age as they can be. Nevertheless, you may be absolutely sure that Granny thinks they are much above normal.

Anyhow, Tink had been trying to find a time when she could entertain Harriet—Tink has such a busy schedule. So she found a time and was having the two of us over to the house for a cookout on the patio at 6:30.

I thought, Why not take the whole day off and just have a diversion? We would doll ourselves up and take our lunch at the club. Then we would come home and rest. About four o'clock, we could have our baths and put on something summery and just sit around and look at magazines or TV until time to go to the cookout.

Harriet said, yes, she thought that would be nice. So we went to the club and got there a minute or two before twelve.

I sat with my back to the big windows so that Harriet would have the pleasure of looking out over the greens.

We had a nice cup of crab bisque, followed by a spinach quiche. The club always has specially good coffee, and we were enjoying our second cup before the girl brought our key lime pie when a certain good-looking young woman came in and took a place about five tables away from us. It was Alice Hollonbrook.

"Guess who just came in," I said.

Harriet took out her compact and pretended to put a little powder on her nose, but really she was using the mirror to observe the new arrival.

"I see," said Harriet. "She's very chic, isn't she?"

And indeed she was. She had on a straight white skirt and a white jacket over a silk blouse striped blue and yellow over gray. She topped it off with a single strand of pearls. As we used to say, ice cream wouldn't melt in her mouth—she was just so collected!

"I hope she didn't do it," Harriet said as she put the compact back in her purse. She was talking about the murder, of course.

I really didn't know the girl in a personal way. But I would have to say that, sitting there, she was a work of art. The way she held the menu, the way she ordered her lunch with lots of sangfroid in a low voice, she could almost have been a princess. On the other hand, it was only art. I really thought I liked the small-town girl better—the one who came to Stedbury for a job. She was natural, you know.

Ten minutes later, another diner made her entrance—not so steady on her feet.

"I wish you would look," I said.

Harriet reached for her purse and had her compact out in a jiffy.

"It is," she said. "Oh Lord, I believe she has been drinking."

Kimberlin Mayburn's costume made a strong contrast to that of Alice Hollonbrook—oh, her clothes were expensive enough and would have been stunning enough if they had been pressed. But she gave the impression of having slept in just what she had on.

Kim selected a table on the far side of the room and slumped into her chair. She took out a cigarette and was vainly trying to get a flame from her lighter when the waitress approached her. Kim glanced at the menu as the lighter at last functioned. She lighted the cigarette, inhaled, and blew out a cloud of smoke.

"I'll have the salmon croquettes." Her voice was quite loud.

Harriet sighed.

"And I'll have another daiquiri," Kim added.

"You just wonder how many she's had," I said.

"Is there somebody," Harriet asked, "that can take over if she goes on with the daiquiris?"

"Well her brother could be summoned—he's a lawyer—lives in the old family place out on the Feganville Road—big old colonial-type house. He's a very decent person—carrying on in the family tradition—well-thought-of—will probably become a judge someday—somewhat uncomfortable in the Democratic party—but loyal to it in the hope that lightning will strike at last."

Harriet and I discussed the present and future prospects of Lawrence Mayburn, Jr., while his sister's daiquiri was brought and consumed.

In the process, there was some conversation between the waitress and Kim—always loud and querulous on the part of Kim.

Meanwhile, Alice Hollonbrook carefully kept her eyes away from Kim.

Knowing what I did about the two women from Harriet's account of her interviews with each of them, it was fascinating to watch Kim, the daughter of one of our oldest families, well on the way to intoxication and not yet aware of Alice's presence. And Alice, the girl from "away," carefully ignorant of the presence of her late husband's mistress. No matter what might have been going through her mind, she was the picture of a perfect lady. The dead Charles Hollonbrook was the link between them—a link that divided.

Suddenly, Kim became aware of Alice. She turned her chair slightly so that she was directly facing the other woman. "Hey!" she exclaimed in that loud, husky voice.

Occasionally, I had been at events where Kim Mayburn was also present, and I recalled that on those occasions her voice had been very attractive—as indeed she herself had been.

"I'm sure poor Alice is in for it now," Harriet said, once more reaching for her compact.

"Hey!" Kim repeated, "I'm talking to you, Mrs. Charles Hollonbrook." Kim got unsteadily to her feet and walked toward Alice's table, with care avoiding the tables and chairs that were in her way.

Every time I see a young woman, pretty and of good family—and Kim Mayburn was both—when I see such a young person drunk and making a display of herself, I think it was better when ladies did not drink as they do now, certainly not alone. But then I am such a back number that I may as well be put into a museum.

"Hey!" Kim said again. "We got something to talk about."

"I don't think so," Alice said.

"When I say we got somethin' to talk about, believe me, lady, we got something to talk about."

"The lawyer for the estate is Dan Blake. He is in the Piedmont Building. He can tell you anything you need to know." Alice was very calm about it. She seemed to be altogether unruffled.

"Well, listen to the little wife!" Kim said.

I dreaded the scene that was developing, although it was very interesting.

"Don't think for a minute that Holly didn't tell me all about you and Clifford Avery," Kim continued.

Apparently, this stung Alice Hollonbrook. Her face was a mask, but a fierce mask, as she said, "Don't think that you were the first woman I had to put up with. And don't think that you would have been the last. Now go back to your table and leave me alone."

Kim swayed slightly as she screwed her face into—well, it was just a leer.

"You thought you could break it up between us," she said.

"Did I?" Alice replied. "It sounds as if you were not sure of him."

"He would have been mine! He would have been mine!" Kim shouted and burst into tears.

Alice called the waitress and told her to get the manager. Once more, Alice was the soul of poise.

Whether Holly loved Alice or not, she was the perfect wife for him. Why would he want Kimberlin Mayburn? For her old family with its past political glory—whatever that amounted to? And there would be a certain amount of money, too. Certainly, he needed that.

I had to admire Alice for the way she was handling this situation. Her behavior seemed always to be so deft. Even in her affair with the man from Baltimore, she had been circumspect. I had not even heard of it until Harriet told me. Of course I don't approve. I don't approve at all. But I am afraid I was on Alice's side.

The waitress scurried around and found the manager very quickly. By the time he had arrived, Kim was hysterical and incoherent.

"Mine, mine! He would have been mine," she kept saying, "in spite of all you could do! You bitch! You jealous bitch!"

The manager was very efficient, very quiet. I suppose he

has had experience in these things. He put his arm over her shoulder and moved her slowly but purposefully out of the room.

The last thing Kim shot back was, "He was mine. You would never have gotten him back."

I looked at Harriet as much as to say, What do you think of that?

She looked at me as much as to say, Very interesting!

We had finished our pie and our coffee and were just sitting there—listening, of course—but my check had not been brought.

I looked up. Alice had stood up and was coming toward us. "I am so sorry you had to be here when all of that went on."

Harriet turned to her. "Darling, you handled it just right. I'm proud of you. Do you know my friend Mrs. Bradfield?"

We acknowledged each other. My check came just then and I signed it. We got up. Harriet patted Alice's shoulder and we walked out. We got into my car and started home, but our thoughts remained at the club as we reviewed the scene we had just witnessed.

Well, we didn't know just what to think about it. It was clear that Kim was on the ragged edge. Such a pity with so much life ahead of her. And what exactly did she mean when she said, "He would have been mine"?

"It could mean anything or nothing," Harriet said. "It merely bears out my hunch. Charles bought that insurance policy in February. That's when he decided to divorce Alice and marry into the Mayburn family for whatever good it would do him. Kim was glamorous—ex of a naval officer—ex of a Frenchman, no matter what kind of rat he may have been—and she had political and family connections.

"So there is enough time between February and May—a little more than three months—for Charles to discover that his new beloved and designated bride is close to the brink.

One thing he doesn't want is a crazy wife. That wouldn't suit his idea at all.

"And it wouldn't be any surprise if little Kim's dear Holly backed off from his plans to divorce Alice. As we have just seen, Alice is the preferable wife—a fashion plate, impressive, tolerant of Holly's frequent and not entirely private peccadilloes, while at the same time she is very discreet in her own little affairs."

"Then you're saying that Holly more or less jilted Kim?" I said.

"I'm just about sure of it."

"And you think maybe she killed him?"

"I have not said that," Harriet replied, "but it could be. Whoever did it would have to be clever. The verdict was suicide. It takes a very cleverly contrived murder to call itself suicide.

"Still, an unbalanced mind can think of things that would never occur to you and me. Think of the meanness and spitefulness and ugly feeling in that little scene the child put on just now. Imagine all of that building up and building up and you needn't be surprised at anything."

I could see Harriet's point. But what a clever person it would take to plan such a murder! Just think of working out an intricate plot and putting it into effect in a distant city, and then think of poor Kim as we had just seen her! Of course, she was drunk, and sober she might be clever. But clever enough to do all that?

"Has Kim got an alibi?" I asked.

Harriet didn't answer. She just looked out the window of the car as I drove along. "I don't know," she said at last. "I failed to ask her. And now I don't see how I am going to."

"It just seems like the authorities ought to be doing this," I said.

Harriet said, "They called it suicide, and sometimes I think that would be the best way to settle the matter. It would have been just fine if I had left it alone. But now I know that either Alice or Kim or both have been done out of five hundred thousand dollars. One or both of them had a right to that money. Besides, there is an unpunished murderer out there."

We went home and took our naps. I don't know about Harriet, but by two o'clock in the afternoon, specially in warm weather, I just get so sleepy, I can't stay awake. Maybe Harriet pondered her problem all afternoon—but not me. My eyes just closed so softly, I hardly knew it; and when they opened again, it was a little past four o'clock.

We bathed and dressed and got to Tink's house a little before six.

Jeff has built a lovely redwood deck on the west side of their house, and there is a big old tulip poplar tree that shades it in the afternoon. It's just the pleasantest place you can imagine.

Tink has garden furniture out there—table and chairs and potted plants all around. She already had the table set. Then, on the lawn she had set up another table and four chairs. The twins were having two of their friends over—a boy and a girl.

Tink explained that there was nothing serious—the boy was Bob's friend and the girl was Ruth's friend, and they happened to be going together. And that arrangement was just fine with Tink.

The young people were on the lawn, throwing their Frisbees and having a wonderful time. Long-legged young people, barefooted, in shorts, brown from a week at the beach; it is just wonderful for my old ears to hear their shouts. And then I thought it might be sad for Harriet because she is all alone. But she smiled and complimented me on my grandchildren. You know, I have six other grandchildren, but I have always been partial to the twins.

We could smell something good cooking in the kitchen, and just then Jeff drove in from the store with a bag of charcoal. He got the grill going. Finally, everything was ready and

Tink called the children in to meet Harriet, and we got down to dinner.

Tink had made cheese grits*—she has this marvelous recipe for it —and green beans and tossed salad, with the steaks done to a turn by Jeff. And then Tink brought out apple pie with homemade vanilla ice cream. We were all pretty full, I can tell you, by the time we finished that meal. The twins' guests went off to see something called *The Horror of New Rochelle* at the "Passion Pit," as the young people call the drive-in movie here. The twins had already seen it and stayed at home. Bob came up and sat on the edge of the deck while Ruth played with the dog.

Harriet got up and dragged her chair over beside Bob.

"Your friends seem very attractive," she said.

I'm sorry to have to report that Bob's "yeah" sounded more like a grunt than anything else.

"Are they in your class at high school?"

"No, we just graduated."

"Have you selected your college?"

"Auburn," he said.

"Will your sister go to Auburn, too?"

"No."

"Where will she go?"

"Salem."

"That's a wonderful school. *Both* of them are wonderful schools. Are you planning to have lots of fun this summer?"

"Yeah."

"I always think the summer between high school and college is the best summer of all."

*Cheese Grits Casserole: Bring 4 cups of water to a boil. Stir in 1 cup quick grits, and cook until real thick. Add 1 stick margarine, 1 cup (4 ounces) shredded Cheddar cheese and 1/8 teaspoon garlic powder. Stir well until the margarine and cheese are melted. In a small bowl beat 2 eggs, and add enough milk to the eggs to make one cup. Stir into grits. Pour into a large greased casserole. Bake at 350°F for 45 minutes to an hour.

Robert seemed to be puzzled by the idea.

"Because," Harriet continued, "you have lots of time to be with your old friends, but you have the fall to look forward to with new experiences, new surroundings, new friends."

Robert seemed to let this soak in.

"I suppose you have lots of friends here in town—I mean from your high school."

"Yeah." Robert's conversation with adults is mostly monosyllables.

"I wonder if you know Jimmy Hollonbrook?" she asked.

"Yeah, I know him."

"I would think he is probably a year or so older than you."

"Yeah, he graduated last year."

"But he's been in town all spring, I think. You wouldn't know where he was on the night of May twenty-sixth, would you?"

"May twenty-sixth?"

There was a pause before the boy went on. "I bet he was still in jail—yeah. See, May twenty-third was our class night. Old Jimmy got polluted at Kelley's and thought the bartender was ripping him off, see. So he started taking the place apart. And that's how he got arrested. Yeah, he was still in jail."

"Bob, I hope you never go into a place like that awful Kelley's," I said. After all, grannies have to preach their sermons.

"Course not," he said, "that place is really rough."

"And you say that was on the weekend?" Harriet asked.

"Yeah."

"On Saturday night?"

"No, on Friday night. See, after he came back from being kicked out of college, the guys he hung out with were mostly high school kids. So Friday night after the dance, a bunch of fellows went to Kelley's."

"How long was he in jail?"

"I don't know. A week."

"No, silly!" Ruth broke in. "They didn't keep him in jail for a week. Just over the weekend."

"I'll bet you a dollar."

"Children, stop it," Tink said. "Act your age."

Harriet then addressed herself to Ruth.

"Do you know exactly when he got out?" she asked.

"No," Ruth replied, "not exactly. But I could ask."

"Ask *him*?" There was a note of surprise in Harriet's voice.

"Not him. I'll ask his girlfriend. She can probably tell what hour he got out."

So Ruth was going to call the girlfriend and let us know the following day.

I VISIT ROSE MOODY

>>Harriet Bushrow<<

I had not seen Tink for twenty years. She always was as pretty as can be, but now that her hair is almost white, she is elegant. I'm so glad she doesn't tint it. And Jeff has put on weight, but not too much. He was skinny when Tink married him. Now he has filled out, and it looks good on him. Poor boy, he's losing his hair. I'll always think of Tink as a child, though she is only thirty-one years younger than I am: That makes Tink fifty-seven.

And those twins—I had never seen them before, you know— just natural, normal young people. They will be in college now for four years, and then suddenly they'll be out in the world, working, contributing, building their own families.

Maud is so fortunate! She has eight grandchildren and three great-grandchildren. When I look at Tink and Jeff, I can't help thinking that Lamar Junior would have been only a little older than they are now if he had lived.

But here I am—alone—not a relative anywhere except for some way-off cousins. So, having no family to be a kind of center to my life, I have to do the crazy things I do. Old folks have to have an interest, something to keep us alive and pro- vide a little zest.

The way I'm going on here, you would think I was rambling. But this is going to get somewhere directly.

Do you remember that Paula Stout said she had gone out to the nursing home and fetched this poor old woman, Rose Moody, home to spend the night with her because it was Moody's birthday?

If you stop to think about it, Paula Stout would be the perfect suspect. She's Hollonbrook's right-hand man, so to speak; and she knew he was going out to make his visits to the different Rotary Clubs and knew where he would be each night. I haven't a doubt but what she made the reservations herself.

She had the key to the Hollonbrook house because she was going to feed the dog and keep an eye on the place—not the kind of thing an office girl would agree to do in this day and time—but it *is* the kind of thing Paula Stout with her good works and deeds and all of that would do.

And with the key to the house and a shrewd guess, she could find the key to the drawer where Charles Hollonbrook kept his pistols and ammunition and silencer and all that. Then there was the note—so easy for her to find down there in the cellar, where it was left for the gun club. Paula would be the perfect suspect if she didn't have that alibi.

That being the case, I thought I would check up on Miss Paula's whereabouts on May 26.

By this time, the reader should be fully aware that Maud Bradfield was just my tower of strength through this whole adventure. It was wonderful that she belonged to the country club and that she is a Baptist, because in a small town down where we live, a Baptist who belongs to the country club knows everybody worth knowing in the whole town. So Maud knew where I could find this Rose Moody. She was at McMenamee's Rest Home.

When people began living so long, there got to be so many of us that taking care of old folks turned into an industry like raising chickens in cages.

McMenamee's Rest Home is right new, and I suppose it is attractive—but not to me. It is situated on a hill on the outskirts of town. It is a beige brick building—only one story so the wheelchairs can roll every which way and the poor old people with their walkers won't be bothered with stairs. There is a large parking lot at the front, and the building is landscaped with pyrocantha and junipers that may do well enough when they get their growth. And there is just window, window, window, one right after the other, each representing a room—like so many post-office boxes.

Well, those little rooms are all the homes the inmates have, and it would be a real work of charity for Paula to provide a little social life for Rose Moody.

There's no porch on the modern rest home. The inside of such places is all shut up and has just the right amount of light and the right amount of heat. The only nature other than human nature in the place is potted plants, and they are plastic.

The interior was bland. There was a reception desk to one side of the hall, but there was nobody there. I could see through to a large room where the television was honking away. Old people were lined up in rows. Wrinkled face after wrinkled face watching what? Geraldo, maybe.

In a little while, a woman in a gray uniform with white stockings and shoes, passing through the room where the old people were, looked over and saw me. She came right away with that kind of rapid, determined step I always associate with nurses. "Care-giver" is probably what they call this woman nowadays. She had a pleasant-enough voice, but I could tell that she was very busy, and I was an interruption.

"Good morning, dear," I said. "I am Ms. Gardner," using my maiden name again just in case—in case of what, I do not know, but it seemed a good thing to do.

"I am visiting here in town and heard that Rose Moody was staying in your lovely rest home. Rose and I were schoolgirls together. I just couldn't leave town without seeing her."

"That's very kind of you," the woman said. She had me sign a register they have for visitors. "I believe Mrs. Moody is here in the television lounge." We were walking toward the big room I had seen. The woman looked around. "I don't see her," she said somewhat surprised, "perhaps she's in her room. Come with me."

I followed just a bit behind the quick, efficient steps of my conductress. Very professional, obviously—professionally alert, professionally cheerful. I wondered what she really felt about her job. Compassion? Probably, but compassion meted out in prescribed doses. A godsend for her charges, no doubt. But for myself, I am resolved to paddle my own canoe as long as the strength is in me.

We went down a long hall, just like a hospital hall, with doors standing partly open. At the end of the hall, my guide stuck her head into a room at the right. "Rose," she said, apparently getting some reaction from the woman within, "we have a visitor."

I went into the room. I would say it was of a very reasonable size. There was a modern metal-frame bed in it and two comfortable-looking chairs, also modern. Then there was this funny-looking old dresser dating back to about 1925—just the wrong time. But, of course, we can't all have beautiful antiques. And I suppose the dresser meant something to Rose Moody, who, I forgot to say, was sitting in one of the chairs. It looked like a church newspaper was in her lap.

"This lady says she knows you." The voice was bright, and I noticed that the matron was speaking just a bit louder. "I'll leave you girls to talk about old times." Then the woman trotted off, her steps as insistent as ever.

"Darling," I said, "it's Hattie Gardner."

Rose Moody peered at me as much as to say, I never saw you in my life. But I was going to convince her that she had.

"It's so good to see your sweet face again," I said as I drew the other chair closer to her and sat in it. "How is your hearing?"

"Why, it's pretty good." And it was a good thing *my* hearing is good, because there wasn't much power behind her voice.

"I notice you are wearing a hearing aid," I said. "How do you like it?"

"It's fine," she said. "It makes a lot of difference."

"Do you like it here at this rest home?" I asked. If we talked long enough and I was positive enough, Rose Moody would begin to think she ought to remember me.

"Pretty well," she said.

My eye fell on her wedding ring and it gave me an idea.

"Maybe you don't know that Lamar passed away," I said.

"Oh, that is so sad," she said in a tone that indicated she had no idea what I was talking about, but there was a sympathetic tone—politeness, of course—and I had to build on that.

"When we are left alone, friends mean so much to us, don't they?" I said.

"Oh my yes," came the answer—just an automatic response.

"I'm visiting here in town, dear," I said, "and I heard you were here. So I thought, I'll go out and see if Rose is still the bright, cheerful little thing I used to have so much fun with."

"It's so good of you to come."

"I understand you had a birthday recently."

"Oh no," she said.

"You didn't have a birthday?"

"Oh yes, I had a birthday, but it wasn't recent. It was last month."

"Well, honey," I explained, "when folks are as old as we are, a month ago is recent. What did you do to celebrate your birthday?"

At this, Rose Moody brightened. "Oh, a young woman from the church came and got me. Took me to her home and gave me a very nice dinner and then we watched the television until nine o'clock."

"Wasn't that lovely," I said. "And then you came back here?"

"Oh no, I spent the night at her house."

"Whose house?"

"This lady from the church. Oh why can't I remember her name?"

"Does she come to see you often?"

"Just now and then. She is very sweet."

"And you spent the night at her house?"

"Yes. I had a very nice room, with the bathroom so convenient."

"I bet you slept well after such a delightful evening."

"Never slept better. Didn't wake up the next morning until nine-thirty."

Well, there I had it. The old fool could be convinced of anything. And with that hearing aid out of her ear, she wouldn't know a thing till the next morning. Paula Stout had undoubtedly entertained this poor woman, but that didn't mean that Paula had an alibi.

When I got back to the house, Maud's little granddaughter had called. They had let Jimmy Hollonbrook out of jail on Monday. That would be the twenty-sixth of May, and he could have killed his father that night—if he was smart enough to figure out how to do it. Which, I might add, I hadn't figured out as yet myself.

So there were a couple more suspects with alibis that weren't alibis at all. After two weeks in Stedbury, I had excavated a ton of dirt, but I hadn't found "who done it" by a long shot.

A VERY
UNEXPECTED EVENT

>> Harriet Bushrow <<

Dogs! It's funny about dogs. Papa always had a collie or two. In the summers they would lie on the porch beside his old rocking chair. Dear old Papa! He was fifty-five, and I thought he was old, old, old.

But dogs! There are three dogs in this story. There was Alice Hollonbrook's cocker, the one that had to be fed—and that was why Paula Stout had the house key and was a suspect. Then there was the mutt that belongs to Maud's grandchildren. It doesn't have anything to do with the story; it was just a dog. But the other dog was important, and I am going to tell about it now.

The fact is, this little dog allowed me to see something that I would not have seen otherwise. When you are raised Presbyterian the way I was, you just have to believe that everything works out the way it is supposed to. And I feel sure this little dog was part of the plan.

But let me explain.

You see, Maud's house is right on the corner—neat little lawn and great big trees along the front but hardly any side lawn at all and no trees there—so that the room where I was staying was practically on the cross street. On the other side of that cross street, there was a house where the lady had a little Chihuahua.

She was just crazy about that Chihuahua—would sit on her patio in back of her house and hold that little dog under her chin, and you'd think she was going to kiss it any minute. And I admit it was cute the way that little thing would run around the yard with its little rear end wiggling until it almost shimmered.

And of course it just went *yap, yap, yap.*

Well this woman's house has a back porch that is screened in, and the little dog has his bed out there. Every time something would wake it up, it would just bark and bark—and if I was sleeping, that would wake me up. Fortunately, Maud lives in a neighborhood where there is very little to disturb a dog.

Well, Maud's garage is so close to the side street that there is scarcely any driveway to it at all. I had to park my old DeSoto on the street, which meant that at night my car was pretty close to the porch where the little dog was sleeping. So I really didn't have to worry about the car with that little dog right there. He was better than a burglar alarm.

Well, as I was coming back to Maud's house after I had my visit with Rose Moody, it was so hot and humid, I could hardly breathe. Maud said surely it would rain. And about 7:30, it did.

Thunder and lightning! Gracious! It was a regular mountain storm. Just buckets of rain! And then it was over and so pleasant and cool that we turned off the air conditioning and opened all the windows.

Maud and I sat there in her living room and reminisced until 9:30 about the girls we used to know at Catawba. And then I retired to my "couch of repose," expecting to enjoy my rest.

It was a fairly bright moon the night after my latest "escapade," and my slumbers were getting along just fine when that little Chihuahua began to yap and woke me up. That scamp was so excited, I couldn't believe he was just barking at an old tomcat. So I reached for my specs on the night table and got up and looked out the window. Parked about ten feet in front of my DeSoto was a big old square-looking van with the motor running. Of course I couldn't tell the color of it, but it must have been a light color because it looked gray in the moonlight.

And there in the light from the street lamp was a hefty man squatting by the side of the DeSoto, pushing something under it. He was there a second, and then as fast as he could he kind of hobbled to his van and jumped in. His motor raced up, and off he took, cutting the corner at the next street so short that his rear wheel went right over the curb.

Then!

All of a sudden there was this brilliant flash under my car and lots of smoke. My ears were deafened with an explosion that shook Maud's house till the teacups rattled. There was another brilliant flash when the gas tank exploded.

"Call nine-one-one," I yelled.

I think Maud was already halfway to the phone.

I threw on my robe, got my dentures in my mouth, and stuck my feet into my slippers. By the time I got out of the house, my poor old car was just a torch.

The woman across the street was having hysterics—thought something had happened to the little dog, I suppose. Other neighbors began to come out.

Then we heard the fire engine whining away and hooting, and the police car, and the little dog yapping as much as ever. We had quite a symphony.

It was so exciting, I hardly had time to think that I had lost my dear old car.

Maud joined me on the sidewalk.

"Oh, Hattie, what happened?" she asked.

"Somebody blew up my car," I said. And that made me think: He blew up my car to tell me to quit nosing around Stedbury, North Carolina.

But it also told me that we were absolutely right about

Charles Hollonbrook's death. Because, you see, there would have been no cause to bomb my car if somebody hadn't wanted to frighten me away; and that person must have been the one who killed Charles Hollonbrook.

Now who was the man that blew up my car?

He had looked to be normally tall—maybe five foot ten or eleven, and he was stocky and ran with a sort of limp. I had the impression that he might have been in coveralls. A working man—painter? plumber? electrician? Some line of work where a man could do his job without being what you might call nimble.

Well, the firemen got there with the hook and ladder truck and I don't know what all. But my old car was already done for. They put out the flames that were burning inside—used chemicals. The poor old thing just looked pitiful. Then the police stood around and watched the firemen.

One of the policemen came over to where we were standing. I must say we looked a fright. My hair was in every direction, but Maud had hers in a net.

"Ma'am," the officer said, "do you know whose car this was?"

Well, he certainly had the right tense of the verb. "It *was* mine," I said.

"I'll have to take down the particulars," he said. "Is there someplace where we can have light?"

Maud had the kitchen light on already. So we just stepped in, and he began asking me about everything—my name and the year and make of the car. That really surprised him. And when I told him it only had forty thousand miles on it, he could hardly believe it.

I told him about the little dog and how it woke me up—and about seeing the man, but I didn't describe him very well because if it sounded like I had recognized him, it was perfectly obvious that next time he blew up anything it would be me. And, of course, I didn't at all see plainly enough to be able to identify the man in a way that would satisfy the police. But I had an idea about his height and build. And then there was the lumbering way he walked. If I saw somebody like that, I made up my mind I'd look at him very closely just on the chance it was the same man.

Maud brewed coffee—sort of an extra-early cup, don't you know. The young policeman was very pleasant and nice. After he had asked me all kinds of things and written down my answers, I said, "And now what is *your* name?"

He was Joe Bell and just as nice as he could be—married and has three little boys—has been on the force for five years—wife comes from Florida.

While he was having the second cup of coffee, Maud said, "After all these years of reading about car bombs—in Northern Ireland and London and all those places—I never would have thought we would have one right here in Stedbury."

"Oh, this wasn't what you would call a 'car bomb,' " the young man said. "Whoever set this one off didn't use anything as fancy as that."

When he looked into our faces and saw how curious we were, he went on: "Monday, we'll have an expert look at the wreckage and determine exactly what explosive was used. But if you ask me, it was blasting gelatin—the same stuff any farmer might use to blow a stump out of his field.

"For this job, I'd say," he went on, "he had about four sticks of that stuff with a cap and a fuse. The fuse sets off the cap, and the cap sets off the gelatin. Then the gelatin sets off the gasoline, and that is it."

After that nice Officer Bell left, Maud and I sat around talking about it quite awhile before we went back to bed. It was just so clear that the explosion and all was a message for me.

Now you might ask how the man knew to blow up the right car. A DeSoto is a landmark in this day and age. I couldn't have been much more obvious if I had rolled into town in a Detroit Electric. Any DeSoto in Stedbury was bound to be my car, and it wouldn't be too hard to find out that I was staying with Maud Bradfield.

I thought about Jimmy Hollonbrook and how interested he had been in my car that day when I pretended it had stalled on me. Could that boy have had something to do with the man that blew up my car? Jimmy thought he was going to have money—lots of it—from his father's estate. All those big houses in Hollondale—if you didn't know that Charles Hollonbrook was just about insolvent, you would think he was big rich. The boy could have offered this man no telling what to come out and dynamite my car. And I had a feeling that Jimmy Hollonbrook would know the kind of folks who would do things like that.

But then, all the other likely suspects had undoubtedly seen my car. So that didn't get me any closer to who the culprit was: Jimmy Hollonbrook, Linda Hollonbrook, Kimberlin Mayburn, Paula Stout—maybe even Alice Hollonbrook—and I couldn't even rule out Ben Rawlings. I had no idea who did it, but all of those people knew about me.

SECOND MEETING OF THE BAKER STREET IRREGULARS

>> Henry Delaporte <<

On Sunday afternoon, I went to the office to work on a brief for a couple of hours. When I returned home, Helen had received a call from Harriet Bushrow in Stedbury, detailing the bombing of her DeSoto. Helen reported that Mrs. Bushrow was cheerful in spite of the loss of her car and her failure to find the thread that would unravel our mystery. If anything, she seemed not only undeterred but more determined than before in her efforts to find the murderer of Charles Hollonbrook.

Helen reported further that Mrs. Bushrow was planning to return to Borderville on Tuesday to tend to some domestic matters, put in a claim for her insurance, and negotiate the purchase of another car.

It is an understatement to say that I was conscience-stricken over the danger to which the Baker Street Irregulars had subjected an eighty-eight-year-old woman by encouraging or even allowing her to investigate a murder. I was, in fact, horrified.

Helen, on the other hand, pointed out that her friend Harriet Bushrow was a free and vigorous spirit who would go her own way and do her own thing, regardless of the Baker Street Irregulars.

"Harriet never fails," Helen assured me. "She will come through."

Nevertheless, at the very least, Rotary had an obligation to Mrs. Bushrow in the loss of her car.

The reader, never having seen the car, may not appreciate its significance. Originally of a blue color, over a period of thirty years it had faded, and a copperish tinge had invaded the blue until the surface was somewhat iridescent in bright sunshine. Mrs. B. kept the vehicle in perfect condition; and why should that not be so? I understand from my wife that Mrs. B. drives only to church, market, and club meetings.

The car is, nevertheless, in use frequently enough that it is one of the local sights of our small city. When it is on the street, it is pointed to, and people say, "That's Mrs. Bushrow. She's still driving that old DeSoto."

There was all the more reason, then, to lay the matter of the DeSoto, its destruction, and Mrs. Bushrow's predicament before the Irregulars.

Accordingly, the Irregulars convened at the close of the next Rotary meeting.

The announcement about the car was a shock to all the men except Fred Middleton, with whom Mrs. Bushrow had also talked by telephone.

The question immediately was what to do about it.

"It's an obligation," Seth declared. Seth Newgent is what I like to think of as the typical Rotarian. There is no subtlety about him, but he volunteers among the first whenever there is a need.

There was a pause after Seth's declaration.

"Well, I suppose it is," Trajan agreed. "What are we going to do about it?"

Old Mr. Garrison had his tobacco pouch out and was filling his pipe. "She still had that old DeSoto!" he said. "I don't suppose there is any possibility of repairing it." He put the pipe in his mouth, struck a match on the bottom of his chair, and got the pipe going with a few loud gurgles.

"No," I said. "The car is a total loss."

"Then we must replace it," J.L. said.

Once J. L. Garrison had said it, the question was not whether it should be done, but how. Some thought the replacement should be paid for out of the club treasury. Others were doubtful that the board would approve so large a sum. It was pointed out that our club had already made contributions to the literacy program, the Boys Club, the Girls Club, the Shelter for Battered Women, the Janie Boyer Home, and the Borderville Ballet.

Finally, J.L. calmed the waters by stating, "This doesn't have to be a new car. Mrs. Bushrow would never think of anything like that. What she needs is a good, nice-looking used car with twenty thousand miles of use left in it. A car like that will last her the rest of her life, and she'll be happy as pigs in the mud."

And so our Irregulars, irregular and unauthorized as we were, created, with me as chairman, along with Leon Jones and Stanley Ferguson, a committee of three to consider what should be done about Mrs. Bushrow's car.

In my new position, I said, "Is there any further business?" I meant it halfheartedly as a joke, but it was also an effort to break up the meeting.

"Yes," Trajan spoke up. "Has Mrs. Bushrow found out anything?"

Knowing that Fred had spoken with Mrs. Bushrow, I looked at him.

"She has quite a list of suspects," he said.

Then it developed that some of the men had an itch to involve themselves in the gumshoe work. Fred agreed to confer with Harriet and see what help she might be able to use.

The meeting of the Irregulars broke up.

Mrs. Bushrow was already in town, having come back from Stedbury that morning. Fred conferred with her and learned that she had some interest in a Bucky Patterson, golf pro at the Playa Grande Club near Lauderdale.

Stanley Ferguson's wife came from Lauderdale. Stan has a brother-in-law down there who is a golfer. Fred got in touch with Stan, and Stan agreed to ask his brother-in-law to investigate.

I RETURN TO
BORDERVILLE

>> Harriet Bushrow <<

Sunday, after Maud and I got back from her church and had our dinner, I tried to call Henry Delaporte, but I got that sweet Helen instead. Well, it's always good to talk to Helen—girl talk, you know. And I told her what had happened so she could report to Henry.

Then I hadn't any more than put down the phone when the police called. There was a bomb expert coming on Monday to examine the remains of my poor old car. They would *prefer* that I leave the car where it was until the expert had seen it.

Leave it there! Did they expect *me* to have it hauled away? I wasn't the one that blew it up. But then, of course, the city didn't blow it up, either. So that left me to pay for the hauling.

I tell you! We learn things every day.

After the expert came on Monday and examined the junk pile that used to be my car, he asked me the same questions that Officer Bell had asked at three o'clock on Friday morning. And all it came to was just that somebody had blown up my DeSoto, which is what I knew without the help of an expert from Raleigh or anywhere else.

But there was one very interesting thing I learned that morning. When the old fellow turned that corner so fast, he left a tire track in the mud. And as luck would have it, the tire had been cut in some way. The police had taken a cast of the track and said they could use the cast to identify the van if they ever found it.

Monday afternoon, I got hold of a man who agreed to haul what was left of the car off. He said he would do it on Tuesday. I wrote a check and left it with Maud. That sweet girl insisted that I not go home on the bus. Her grandson—Robert, you remember—was going to drive her car, and he and I would go to Borderville on Tuesday morning. Then he would bring the car back to Stedbury in the afternoon.

And that is what we did.

Now it takes an hour and a half to drive from Stedbury to Borderville, and you remember what a chatterbox that boy is from my "conversation" with him when Tink Smith had that lovely cookout for me: "yeah" . . . "uh-huh" . . . and "yeah" again. He's a good-looking boy, but I'm afraid he hasn't developed his powers of conversation yet.

I guess that was why I was determined to draw him out. "Drag him out" would be more like it.

"Robert, do you have a girlfriend?"

"Yeah."

"Is she pretty?"

"Uh-huh."

"I bet she's a blonde with pretty blue eyes."

"Naw, brown hair."

"Did you take her to the senior prom?"

"Uh-huh."

Lord have mercy! I tried everything I could think of to get that boy to talk. He is seventeen and I am eighty-eight. I was beginning to think that "never the twain shall meet" when it just popped up that the boy was crazy about hunting.

Well now, Lamar was quite a hunter and I used to go hunting with him once in a while, so I knew how to talk the language.

And when Robert heard that I once shot a ten-point buck, the difference of age melted away like a fog in July.

I almost wished I hadn't mentioned it. I heard all about .20-20 rifles and six-gauge shotguns and this kind of sight and that kind of sight and what he was going to buy with his birthday money.

Now I have read about these animal-rights people that object to testing drugs on animals and hunting and all that. Well, I just want to ask them whether it isn't better for a boy to shoot rabbits and squirrels than for him to shoot dope. Not that Robert went out and shot rabbits and squirrels. He was way past that: He and his father shot ducks in season and he got a wild turkey once.

Robert—that tongue-tied boy—nearly talked my left ear off. There was somebody named Larry who kept being mentioned.

"Is this Larry one of your friends in your school?" I asked, just to be polite. After all, I was the one who got the boy started on this conversation."

"In my school!"

Obviously, I had asked a very stupid question.

"No, he's not in school."

There was a pause that seemed to say that any fool would know about Larry.

"Larry Mayburn is a big lawyer. His dad was Senator Mayburn. Of course he's not in school."

You know what the Bible says about the mouths of babes and sucklings. Robert was no babe or suckling, but something had come out of the child's mouth that alerted me like an electric shock.

"Does this Larry," I asked—almost afraid Robert would say no—"does he shoot pistols, too?"

"Jeez! Does he!"

Maud would not have approved of that boy's profanity—but, you see, he had forgotten for just a minute that I was his grandmother's chum, and I took it for a compliment.

So there it was. Larry Mayburn was a pistol enthusiast, and he was Senator Mayburn's son, and Senator Mayburn was Kimberlin Mayburn's father. So that made Kimberlin and Larry brother and sister.

"I don't suppose you would know if this Larry was a friend of Mr. Charles Hollonbrook?" I held my breath for the answer.

"Yeah."

"And did he shoot on Mr. Hollonbrook's pistol range that is in Mr. Hollonbrook's basement?"

"Yeah. And he took me down there one time and let me shoot his P Thirty-eight—that's a real old German pistol that was used back in World War Two."

Yes, World War Two is "real old." I wondered what Robert would think if I told him I remember the days when we prayed for the "boys in France," and that was World War One.

By the time I got through thinking about that, I realized that Robert was going on about the pistol range in the Hollonbrook basement.

"Mrs. Hollonbrook showed me the pistol range when I visited her," I said.

For a second, the boy took his eyes off the road and looked at me in astonishment. Then he turned back to his driving.

"Yes," I continued, "Mrs. Hollonbrook showed me her husband's gun collection and everything." Robert was silent. Obviously, I had stunned him.

"Did you like Mr. Hollonbrook?" I asked.

"Gosh yes! He said I could come back sometime and use the range. But now . . ."

The young are much more in awe of death than old folks are. The thought of my own death doesn't bother me at all—though I'm not exactly eager for it. But the thought of Hollonbrook's death gave Robert a moment of reflection.

"Now," he took up his observation again, "I guess I won't get to use it." Then he volunteered, rather quietly, "Mr. Hollonbrook was a real neat guy."

"Neat?" I asked. "How do you mean, neat?"

"You know, cool."

There it was in the words of youth—neat and cool—Charles Hollonbrook, the charmer who seemed able to invite himself into almost any young woman's bed—the salesman who could come into a strange town and establish himself immediately—the businessman who could bring an enterprise like Featherstone Plastics to Stedbury, North Carolina and get himself elected to Rotary and be district governor—of course such a man was neat and cool. Look at him through a boy's eyes; look at him through the world's eyes. Could he have wished to take his own life? On the other hand, could anybody have wished to kill him? Neat! And cool!

When we got to my house and Robert had deposited my hatbox and suitcase in my bedroom, I said, "Now, Robert, we can eat wherever you want to. We can eat at the Inn or at the Pizza House, or Sizzling Steak, or McDonald's." And do you know, he wanted to eat at McDonald's!

So as soon as I got him started back over the mountain, I called his grandmother.

"Maud," I said, "you didn't tell me all there is to know about Larry Mayburn."

"Oh, I didn't?" she said apologetically. "I guess I just didn't think about it."

Now that was poor, and I told her so. Then she explained the whole thing.

Judson Mayburn—the *old* man (and that puts him back in the last century)—married a Miss Tuckahee from Granite Falls. Her family didn't have much, but they were very fine people. This first wife had one daughter, who married a man from Denver and lives out there.

Then, when that Mrs. Mayburn died, Judson Mayburn married again, and Julia Hartley was his second wife. The Hartleys had mills over in the central part of the state. So the second wife had money. And she also had two children: Kimberlin and Lawrence, who were much younger than Senator Mayburn's older daughter. Since the second Mrs. Mayburn was of independent means, old Judson Mayburn, when he died, left the bulk of his estate to his elder daughter, expecting the second wife's money to come to his children by her. And it did— enough of it that neither Kim nor Larry had to worry about whether it would ever stop coming.

Maud had not made the connection between Larry Mayburn and Charles Hollonbrook. But, of course, Larry Mayburn was just the man to be a friend of Charles Hollonbrook.

"Maud," I said, "call your Pete Gambrill, the one who fixes your heat pump, and ask him whether Larry Mayburn had a key to Charles Hollonbrook's basement."

Thirty minutes later, Maud called back. Yes, Lawrence Mayburn had a key.

"Now one other thing," I said. "Is Lawrence Mayburn heavyset?"

Maud said no, and then she said yes, and finally she said, "Well, you might say so."

I knew right then that as soon as I got my insurance money for the DeSoto and I could manage to get myself a new car, I would have to go back to Stedbury and take a look at Mr. Lawrence Mayburn.

THOSE SWEET BOYS IN ROTARY

>> *Harriet Bushrow* <<

Coming home the way I did without my car, I found myself in a regular pickle. A package of Maxwell House and a box of corn-bread mix was about all the groceries I had in the house— and no way to get to the store. I had to impose on my neighbor across the street to take me in her car so I could buy enough to eat for at least a week—being without transportation, you know.

Of course, I've done little things for her like taking in the mail and feeding her cat and so on whenever she was away from home. Still, I wanted to get my insurance straightened out right away so as not to be a burden on her any longer than necessary.

So on Wednesday, as soon as my agent's office opened, I called him and told him my car had been blown to bits.

What a shock I had! All the company would give me was two hundred fifty dollars.

Now I have my Social Security, and Lamar left me an annuity and a few stocks. And I own my little house, and I just love it. But I don't have a lot of money.

The taxi service in Borderville is terrible and the bus is even worse—inconvenient at best—and waiting on the corner in the wet and the cold is not going to be good for my old bones. I didn't see how I could afford a new car, at least not right away. The thought entered my mind that I might be about ready for a retirement home. Then I thought about that poor Rose Moody at McMenamee's Rest Home. And I would have to give up my beautiful furniture—and not a relative left to give it to! I was pretty blue, I can tell you.

Then the telephone rang. It was that precious Helen Delaporte. She is such a thoughtful thing. She was calling to see if I had gotten home all right, and she offered to run any errands I might have.

So you see, the ravens come, after all. But I couldn't be imposing on my friends all the time. I told Helen my troubles. She was so sweet about it—said to call on her anytime.

Now I couldn't do that, could I?

But it was darling of her to offer, and we always feel better knowing friends are thinking of us. So I poked around the house feeling halfway sorry for myself until Friday, when the phone rang and it was Henry Delaporte.

"Mrs. Bushrow?" I knew his voice right away.

"Why, Mr. Delaporte! So nice of you to call!"

"The Baker Street Irregulars have been concerned about your car."

I didn't quite understand what he meant by "Baker Street Irregulars" until he explained. Then he went on.

"I am handling the estate of Mrs. J. F. Foster, and she had a 1982 Buick Skylark with only fifty-eight thousand miles on it. It's a clean car, and as far as I can tell it is in good mechanical condition. I can let you have it for what the dealer has offered us."

Wasn't that lovely!

That sweet boy wouldn't let me decide about it until he could show it to me and let me drive it. So he brought it around to the house right away. It was shiny as new—a light tan, almost gold in color—had radio and air conditioning—just everything I could want.

He said he thought the brakes might need tightening, but he would see to that. And with the insurance from the DeSoto, I would have to pay just four hundred dollars.

I was delighted and said I certainly would take it and wanted to write the check right then.

"Now, are you sure you really want it?" he asked.

I said, "Yes!"

And then he said, "Since you are satisfied with this car and you lost your DeSoto in carrying on an activity that we asked you to undertake, the Baker Street Irregulars are giving you this Buick."

Now could there be anything nicer than that! But that's the way Rotarians are. Oh, of course, there are those big international projects like the Rotary Foundation and all of that. But there are so many local needs that they supply. Those men just have wonderfully big hearts.

Then Henry Delaporte drove off in my new car, transferred the title for me, got the license, had the brakes adjusted and the car completely serviced. When he brought it to me the next day, the tank was full of gas.

Now Henry must have paid for that part of it out of his own pocket.

After all of that, I began to feel ashamed of myself. Here I had put the Irregulars to expense, not to mention poor Maud, who had had to put up with me for almost two weeks—not that it hadn't been fun for both of us, but I'm sure she had other things to do, and my being there—well you are always glad to see company come and to see it go.

But be that as it may, now that I had a car, I just had to go back down there to Stedbury. Knowing that Maud thought Larry Mayburn, Kim's brother, might be heavyset and that he had a key to Charles Hollonbrook's basement—I was just sure that if I could see him—and especially see him walk—I would be pretty sure, lawyer or not, whether he had blown up my old DeSoto.

So I sat down and wrote to Maud.

> *You Precious Girl,*
> Although I talked to you twice on the phone, I don't think I halfway expressed my pleasure and gratitude on account of your hospitality. Our hair may be gray and our bodies full of aches and pains, but when we are together it seems like all of that melts away.
> The loveliest thing! Those sweet men in the Rotary Club found a car for me—a nice Buick with everything—windows that go up and down at the press of a button—everything! I feel very sporty and up-to-the-minute when I drive around in it.
> Darling, I'm going to impose on you, but I just must get a look at that Larry Mayburn. If he should only turn out to be the man who threw that dynamite under my car, I feel I could clear up the whole mystery.
> So this is what I was thinking. If there is some occasion that he is likely to attend—like a public banquet or something, let me know, and I'll drive down, look at him, and come right back home. I won't be such a bother to you this time. But I just have to know if Larry Mayburn is my man.
> Maud, that grandson of yours, that Robert! Aside

from being the handsomest thing, he is just as nice as he can be—kept me entertained all the way home from Stedbury. Guns, guns, and more guns—Ha! Ha! Well, I just want to do something for that boy because he was so sweet to me. I'm going to send him a copy of *The Famous DAR Murder Mystery* and get all the Daughters that worked on it to sign their names.

Now I'm not going to stay with you any longer than overnight this time. Just let me know when it would be the right time.

Affectionately,
Harriet B.

Ten days later, I got an answer from Maud.

Dear Hat,

The idea of your saying you would come to Stedbury and stay only one night! Come and stay as long as you like, whenever you like. You have no idea how your visit pepped me up. And the mystery is more exciting than ever. The "demolition" of your car made a "big noise" in Stedbury. My Sunday-school class had a party on Thursday, and all anybody could talk about was *your* car.

Your letter didn't get here until Wednesday—that's what happens when you mail something over the weekend—and I happened to think that there was a dance at the club on Friday night. Tink and Jeff were going to be there and the twins would go with them. I thought, Well! I'll have Robert take his new camera he got for graduation and take pictures of Lawrence Mayburn.

Well, Mayburn was there, all right, and Robert took

pictures. Some of them are blurred, but three or four are very clear. So I'm sending them along. Maybe you can identify the "bomber" from these.

Love,
Maud

The pictures were clear enough. But they were not pictures of the man who blew up my car.

BAKER STREET IRREGULARS, III

>> *Fredrick M. Middleton* <<

With the return of Harriet Bushrow to Borderville, the interest of the Baker Street Irregulars may be said to have reached a plateau. Since our agent had not yet cracked the case, we were somewhat in the position of football fans whose team has returned home after tying a game. The team is no nearer the conference championship, but the hopes of the fans are by no means dashed.

So there we were, all ten of us, at the close of the last club meeting in June, and Henry Delaporte had a letter from our operative. It began:

> Dear Baker Street Irregulars,
>
> A detective—at least a lady detective—operates on intuition, and my intuition tells me that Mr. Henry Delaporte, and undoubtedly some other "Irregulars," had more than a passive role in securing for me the beautiful Buick car that replaces my old DeSoto. If my intuition is right, I want to express my thanks. It was a lovely thing that you did.

As a matter of fact, each of us chipped in one hundred dollars, and the car cost a good deal more than our friend will ever guess, but we'll let that pass. The letter continued:

> In view of the support you have given me, it is only right that I should give you a resume of what I now know about the death of your district governor, Charles Hollonbrook, on May 27.
>
> First, I cannot stress too strongly that we are dealing with a case of murder, as is proved by the violent reaction to my investigations expressed when my car was blown to bits. With this fact established, we must consider the possible motives for the murder of the late district governor.
>
> Unfortunately, the facts that I have turned up regarding Mr. Hollonbrook do not reflect credit upon him, and the publication of them will very likely cause embarrassment to your club and others in your district. However, I beg you to keep in mind that very few men are murdered without reason.
>
> The facts which I have been able to ascertain have led me to identify at least six possible suspects. For your consideration, I list them below.
>
> 1. Victor Douglass—college friend and former business partner, from whom Charles Hollonbrook received many favors and much assistance—was cheated out of a substantial profit and reduced in circumstances by the breakup of the firm of Hollonbrook and Douglass.
>
> 2. Mrs. Linda Hollonbrook and her son, James Hollonbrook. Mrs. Hollonbrook never overcame the bitterness of her divorce, insisted that her former husband had been unjust to his children, and expected them to gain affluence from his death. James

Hollonbrook had access to his father's guns and memo pads identical to the one from which the paper for the so-called suicide note was taken. The boy knew of his father's whereabouts on May 26. Furthermore, James Hollonbrook's behavior indicates a tendency to violence. No alibi.

3. Mrs. Alice Hollonbrook—alienated by her husband's frequent infidelities—was conducting an affair with a married man at the time of Hollonbrook's death. The gentleman friend—who seems unwilling to divorce his wife for financial reasons—is Mrs. Hollonbrook's unreliable alibi. Mrs. Hollonbrook had access to the pistol and silencer, the memo pads, and her husband's whereabouts. On the other hand, Mrs. Hollonbrook stood to lose $500,000 of insurance money if her husband died by suicide. She appears to have been aware that her husband's estate was seriously depleted.

4. Ms. Kimberlin Mayburn, twice divorced, somewhat unbalanced mentally, was Mr. Hollonbrook's most recent conquest. It seems likely that the gentleman was contemplating divorce from his wife and marriage to the suspect. There is also the possibility that Hollonbrook, aware of Mayburn's instability, may have withdrawn from the affair recently. Mayburn's brother had access to Hollonbrook's guns and perhaps notepads. Mayburn can be assumed to have known of Hollonbrook's whereabouts on May 26.

5. Ben H. Rawlings of the Estonia Savings and Loan. Hollonbrook for some time had been blackmailing Mrs. Rawlings and receiving unwarranted loans from Estonia Savings to finance his real estate development. With the decline of real estate business in Stedbury, Hollonbrook was unable to pay his debts, and because of blackmail the Estonia Savings

was deterred from foreclosure. Rawlings was in Boone, North Carolina, within easy reach of Borderville on the night of the murder.

6. Paula Stout—"angel of mercy" or "the world's doormat"—as secretary-treasurer of the Hollonbrook firm, she may have expected to gain by Hollonbrook's death. She had access to the gun and silencer, the notepad, and Hollonbrook's complete itinerary. Her alibi can perhaps be rejected, and there seems to be a harsher side to her character than that of the cheerful doer of good deeds.

7. Also ran: Buchannan Patterson. Hollonbrook caused Patterson's divorce from his wife, Desiree, and had him fired from his job as golf pro at the Stedbury Country Club. Patterson's involvement occurred some time ago and his present employment, in Florida, places him at too great a distance from Borderville. He seems not to be a very likely candidate.

There are others who had access to the gun and perhaps to the memo pads. The above list of suspects represents the status of my investigations when my car was destroyed. Obviously, the man who exploded my car is also a suspect, whoever he is.

I trust that you gentlemen will agree that I have been diligent in my investigation. At the moment, I am considering how best to proceed.

Faithfully yours,
Harriet Gardner Bushrow

There was a brief silence before Seth Newgent said, "Who would think that a little old lady could find out all that stuff and put it into a report like that?"

"Anyone who has been playing bridge with her for twenty years, as I have, would think of it," I said.

"By the way," Stan Ferguson said, "you can leave the golf pro out of the picture. My brother-in-law in Lauderdale tells me Buck Patterson is back with his wife. However, and this is the joker, he is now the pro at the Poplar Hill Club."

"He is!" Henry looked at Stan in surprise, as we all did. "I'll pass that on to Mrs. Bushrow." Poplar Hill is only forty miles from Borderville.

"It's the mistress who did it," Leon Jones said. "It's always the mistress in a slinky nightgown—or maybe the wife. But it's got to be a slinky nightgown."

Then Leon was barraged with comments like, "What kind of TV do you watch?"

Finally, Trajan got us back in order by moving that the Baker Street Irregulars express appreciation to Mrs. Bushrow and encourage her to continue the good work.

With a chorus of approval, the Irregulars adjourned and straggled out of the room.

IMPORTANT DISCOVERY IN BORDERVILLE

>> Harriet Bushrow <<

I have always known I ought to have my head examined. Anybody with any sense at all would quit and go home when her car was dynamited. She ought to know the same thing could happen to *her* that happened to the car. Well, I did, in fact, go home, but I just couldn't quit. Curiosity killed the cat, but cats have nine lives, and they don't die easily.

After I got caught up on all the things that happened in the neighborhood—I had to do that, you know—and after I got my housekeeping straightened out, I found that I was just sitting around doing nothing but thinking about that case.

All along I had said that once I knew who the murderer was, I would go on to figure out how he—or she—or they—did it. I had been close enough to the murderer, or his or her cooperator, to get my car blown up, and still I could take my list of suspects and say that any of them could have done it. Maybe if I turned my attention to how it was done, that would tell me which one of my suspects was the man—or the woman.

So I dressed up—hat and gloves, best shoes, the works—got into my nice new car, and drove over to the Borderville Inn. I sailed into the lobby and informed the young man at the desk that my son and his wife with their daughter and her husband along with their three children were coming to visit me and I just didn't feel that I could keep all that managerie in my house and retain my wits. Would he be so kind as to let me inspect the accommodations the Inn had to offer.

"Why, certainly, madam."

He called for another young man, gave him a key, and instructed him to show me whatever I wanted to see. The second young man led me to the first room on the left as you go toward the swimming pool. That was not the room where the murder took place; it was five doors down from the room where the murder took place; but as all the rooms are exactly alike, it didn't matter which room I examined.

Like the murder room, this room had two double beds—blond oak headboard—two armchairs, one chest of drawers, a surface to put your bags on, a mirror, one straight chair, a round table, a kind of night table with drawers in it and a light attached to the wall beside it, and a TV. The door and a plate-glass window with draw curtains made up one side of the room. The opposite end of the room contained an alcove with basin and mirror. On one side of the alcove, a door opened to the bath. On the other side was a closet with louvered doors that folded back. I suppose someone could have hidden in the closet for a short while or in the bathroom. And even if someone used the toilet, another person could be hidden in the tub, behind the shower curtain. But nobody could hide longer than just a few minutes that way without being discovered.

I went around looking at everything—tested the mattresses with my hand, flushed the commode, looked in the drawers, ran my gloved finger along horizontal surfaces to inspect for dust. I asked if the walls were fireproof. The poor man who was showing me the accommodations must have thought I was very concerned for cleanly and comfortable accommodations for my mythical family.

Finally, I got around to what I really wanted to see—the lock on the door and the chain arrangement that they had had to break when they burst into Charles Hollonbrook's room a month before.

Actually, the "chain" was a loop of brass—U-shaped—attached by a plate screwed into the door in such a way that the loop swivels back and forth. Then on the doorjamb, there is a projecting hook attached firmly to the jamb with screws. This hook is rigid and ends in a knob a bit larger than the diameter of the hook.

When the door is closed, the brass loop can be placed over the hook. The door can then be opened slightly, but the loop, being caught by the hook, prevents the door from opening further.

The widest opening of the door allowed by the loop is no more than an inch. It would be impossible to put a hand through this crevice, and I could not imagine how the link of the "chain" could be disengaged from the outside.

I worked the mechanism several times and was very pleased with the outcome of my inspection. I walked with the young man back to the lobby, thanking him profusely.

As he gave the key back to the gentleman at the desk, I said, "When I was here some time ago, I met a very beautiful young lady—a Miss Teddy Brazille. How is she?"

"She is not with us any longer," the young man said.

"Not with you? Why, where did she go?" At that point, I had an intimation that I had stumbled onto something.

"She just suddenly quit. Went to New York."

"My goodness," I said. "What will she do for money?"

"I think she came into some," he said. "From an aunt."

"Her aunt died and left it to her?"

He frowned. "No, I think she gave it to her."

"And this rich aunt—who is she?"

"Don't know. Someone down there in North Carolina where Teddy came from."

"Stedbury?" I held my breath.

"Yeah, I believe that's it."

Well, that was something to think about, and I thought about it all the way home and all through the evening until I fell asleep in bed, and I was thinking about it again in the morning when I first woke up.

Ah, but a man's reach should exceed his grasp,
Or what's a heaven for?

That was one of the things Miss Langrock had us memorize at Catawba Hall. It's funny how those things come back to us across the years.

I had grasped some things, and I was reaching for others. I had grasped how Charles Hollonbrook had been killed with his own gun in a locked room. I did not yet grasp the answer to the question of who did it. But I was reaching, and I would soon have it.

And yet, although I would soon know all the answers to my own satisfaction, proving any of it was another matter.

I am not a feminist, and I have never felt at a disadvantage because I am a woman. I have always thought it was a privilege to be a woman—and for men it is a privilege to be a man. Nevertheless . . .

Nevertheless, I knew there wasn't a man living who would listen to me unless I could prove to an absolute certainty that what I said was *so*. Not only am I a woman but I am an *old* woman. Who's going to listen to a dotty old woman the likes of whom *I* wouldn't even listen to?

But I knew how to get just a few more bits of information, and then I would know how to convince the authorities and bring the culprit to justice.

As soon as I had washed my breakfast dishes, I dialed Maud.

"Who," I said right off the bat, "is Theodora Brazille?"

Maud told me right away.

"Why didn't you tell me that before?" I asked.

"Because you didn't ask," she said.

I declare, I felt like an absolute dumbbell. All those hours I had spent snooping around about this one and that one—I could have done without all of that if I had just asked the right question at the very first.

I told Maud I would be in Stedbury as fast as I could—just as soon as I had taken care of a few things around the house. "We'll get this thing settled in a few days," I promised. Maud was about as excited as I was. It was a wonderful feeling.

>>*Harriet Bushrow*<<

If I ever do any more detecting, I'm going to make them give me a secretary to write it up afterward. Doing the detecting and all of that is fun. But I have never learned to type, and it gets awful tiresome writing all this out by hand. But we are getting on toward the end now.

The next morning after I arrived in Stedbury, I called Alice Hollonbrook as soon as etiquette would permit. "Dear," I said, "if you're not too busy this morning, there is something I need to talk about." She said that would be fine, and I went right over.

The poor child seemed very glad to see me, and she was even gladder when I told her I felt sure she would be able to collect on the life insurance in the near future. This was specially welcome news, because Dan Blake, her lawyer, had notified her that Estonia Savings and Loan had started foreclosure proceedings.

"After that," she said, "the rest of the estate will be so little and divided among so many that it will be like nothing."

It would be a comedown for her. She had gone so far and learned such expensive tastes. How much better if she had married into something more stable! But everyone to her own fancy.

I told her about my interview with Ben Rawlings. She was very much surprised about dear Holly's getting his loans through blackmail, although she knew he had continued to get those loans long after he was in a serious financial scrape. If Lamar had had trouble like that, he would have told me all about it, and we would have gone through it together. But then, Lamar was one in ten million.

I said I hoped she didn't mind that I had given the clipping to Mr. Rawlings, and she said she was glad I did it. I believe Alice Hollonbrook had good intentions from the beginning, but she could hardly live in that environment without being influenced for evil as well as for good.

At last I got down to what I really wanted to know.

"Darling, I hope you won't be offended," I began, "but when we had our chat before, I believe you said you were not the cause of your husband's divorce. Still, I can't believe you were never intimate with Holly until after he separated from his wife."

"We had a relation," she said, "but Linda did not know about it until later."

I had my doubts about this, but I let it stand. "And did you ever spend the night with him in a motel? I mean, before you were married?"

She almost laughed in my face.

I put my hand on her knee and said, "I have a reason for asking the questions in this way. The next thing is—after you had your little 'relation,' did he take a sleeping tablet, roll over, and go right to sleep?"

Her eyes flashed. "How did you know?"

"There, there," I said, "just tell me if I am right."

"Yes. It used to hurt me the way he suddenly lost interest. Then it made me mad. He laughed at me—said I ought to be practical—that he had to have his sleep, because so many people make a racket leaving a motel in the morning."

"And would you think the same thing would happen if he took some other woman to a motel for a 'relation'?"

"Yes."

Well, there I had it. He took sleeping pills whenever he spent the night in a motel—with or without a mistress. And any woman who had had very many rendezvous with him at motels would know all about his little habits.

I was very pleased with this brief interview. On the way back to Maud's house, in my mind I went on to the next thing. It was only a guess, but I thought it was a reasonable guess. You see an operator—a sexual operator—but then I'm not supposed to know about that sort of thing.

Anyhow, it was most fortunate that Jay Bradfield had been an insurance man—very successful. And the gentleman who has the agency now—Pelham Stafford is his name—was Jay's partner.

So Maud knew a lot about the insurance office, and we talked it all over and put two and two together and got the right answer. Maud called Pel on the phone at his home that evening and explained what we wanted. He knew the answer right off. Of course, it was office information and confidential, but when Maud explained the situation to him, he gave her the information.

Then Maud put me on the phone. It was a little difficult explaining what I wanted him to do, but he finally saw what I was up to, and he gave me an appointment for ten o'clock the next morning.

When I went into the insurance office, I announced myself in a good strong voice. "I am Mrs. L. Q. C. Lamar Bushrow," I said. Everybody on the block could have heard me.

Mr. Stafford was ready for me, and the young woman escorted me to his office.

"Mrs. Bushrow," he said apologetically, "I can't imagine Nellie Penn letting out confidential information. But as you explained it, it is very suspicious. And as you say, your little scheme will prove whether she did or did not do it." With that, he called his secretary on the office intercom.

"Nellie, will you please bring the complete file on the Hollonbrook policies."

He released the button, and immediately Miss Penn's voice came on. "All of them?"

"Yes, *all* of them."

Within seconds, the office door opened and a somewhat nondescript person came in. I saw immediately that her eyes were apprehensive, although that may have been my imagination. "Miss Penn," he said, "this is Mrs. Bushrow, the lady who solved the DAR murder mystery. I am sure you have heard of her."

"How do you do," she said none too cordially as she handed the file to Mr. Stafford.

"Mrs. Bushrow hopes to prove that Chuck Hollonbrook was murdered." He paused and gave his secretary an inquiring look. "That would allow Mrs. Hollonbrook to collect on her policy."

There was a brief but awkward silence. Then Miss Penn was dismissed and left the room.

Mr. Stafford did not open the file but laid it on the desk. "The information that I gave you on the phone yesterday is correct, Mrs. Bushrow," he said. "I'll lock this file in my desk drawer. I have the only key."

I left Mr. Stafford's office about 10:20. That would give Nellie Penn an hour and forty minutes in which to stew before her lunchtime. I was very pleased with myself. I thought I had baited a trap pretty well.

But a baited trap does not always spring on its prey immediately. In fact, two days went by. Then on Friday, the phone rang for me.

It was a muffled voice. I was not sure whether it was a man trying to talk like a woman or a woman trying to talk like a man, but I was betting on a man rather than a woman.

The voice, of course, wanted to know whether I was Mrs.

Bushrow. And when that was out of the way, there were only two sentences—and I'll remember them till I die—which won't be very far off now. The voice said, "If you want to learn who killed Mr. Hollonbrook, meet me at the bandstand in the park on Black's Mill Road tonight at eight o'clock. Come alone." That was all.

Black's Mill Road.

Maud explained that the city had a park at the edge of town. They never really took care of the park very well, but there was a baseball diamond out there, where the church teams and all that practiced and played their games. But more recently, the Dad's Club had put in lights on the field at the high school because the effluent from Featherstone Plastics has so polluted Black's Creek that the old ball field is no longer popular.

So the park would be deserted by eight even though it wouldn't be quite dark then.

"You must not go over there," Maud said.

"I'd like to know why not!" I said.

She said there was a road on the back side of the park that was used for access, but that with the pollution and chug holes in the Black's Mill Road hardly anybody ever used it unless absolutely necessary. And all along the creek, the banks are grown up in brush and trees and weeds.

"Why they could grab you and drag you into those bushes and no telling what they would do to you."

Well, that made me stop and think. I wanted the man—yes, it would have to be the man—the one with that blasting gelatin—to make some kind of move so I could identify him and connect him with what had happened to my car, which would also connect him with the murder. And here he had made his move. Now that I was face-to-face with the thing I had been hoping for—don't you see—it was just too scary.

I had thought about the danger before I left home, and I had taken Lamar's revolver and some shells out of the right-hand drawer of my secretary bookcase. So I had put that in my suitcase.

Well, I had this opportunity to identify the man, and I just couldn't let it slip through my hands. I told Maud about the pistol. I would have it right there in my purse, which was a good-sized purse, and I felt sure I still knew how to shoot if I found it necessary.

She wouldn't have any of that. She wanted to call the police.

I said, "Absolutely not!"

She wanted to know why not.

In the first place, the police would never believe an old woman who said there was somebody lying in wait for her down by the creek. And in the second place, they wouldn't let me go down there if they believed it. And in the third place, if a police car came anywhere near the park, the man wouldn't show up and the officers would just laugh at us. And there wasn't a fourth place, because I wasn't going to call any police.

If there had ever been any chance that I would back down and not be at that park at eight o'clock, by the time I got through with all those first, second, and third places, that chance was gone and the matter was settled.

Dinner was not very pleasant that night. Maud was just sure I was eating my last meal. She didn't say so, but I knew that was what she thought. And the fact is, I wasn't very hungry myself.

Well, I got out there. The sun had already sunk below the big old dark trees along the creek. It was about the dreariest place you ever want to see.

There was a parking lot for the cars—none there, of course—weeds coming up through the gravel except where oil had leaked. I pulled my car in and got out.

Should I lock it or not? It was not the place to leave an unlocked car, and I wasn't sure the Baker Street boys would be best pleased if I lost this Buick. But on the other hand, I might want to get into the car in a hurry. So I left it unlocked and put the keys in my purse, taking the opportunity to look at my revolver, just for comfort. I said, "Lord, if you'll see me through this one, you can do as you please next time."

Isn't that awful!

Well, to go on about that park. Over to the left were some ramshackle bleachers by the baseball diamond, and over in the other direction I could see some swings and slides for the children. Directly ahead of me was the bandstand, and not too far from that was a small brick building.

I saw no sign of the man I had come to meet. But there were some benches around the bandstand and some bushes, so I couldn't see whether the benches were all empty or whether someone might be sitting there hidden by one of the shrubs.

The man had said I was to meet him by the bandstand, which meant, I supposed, I would have to go over there if I expected to see him.

So I started out walking over the grass toward the bandstand. I'm sure my heart was beating faster than it had done in a long, long time.

I was about halfway to the bandstand, I suppose, when I felt I just had to look behind me. And there, crossing the road, was the big old lumbering figure of a heavyset man. Yes, it was the man I had seen throw that blasting gelatin under my DeSoto.

It's all very well to be brave when you are sitting in Maud's living room telling her you don't want the police, but when you're alone in that huge, vacant park with a creature like that behind you, it's different.

I quickened my pace. After all, I had done what I had wanted to do. I had seen the man clearly enough to identify him. But now I was not quite sure I knew *what* to do.

I quickened my pace still more and looked back again. Then I realized why the man had such a lumbering walk: He was lame.

Well, that gave me hope. An old lady eighty-eight years old

can't run very fast, but maybe she could keep ahead of a lame man. So I began to run.

I got almost to the bandstand when I thought I had better take my gun out of my purse. I was fumbling around with that and not paying enough attention to where I was going, and suddenly my foot went into a rabbit hole and I fell to my knees. Fortunately, my fall was softened by the thick grass, and I didn't break anything. But the man gained on me as I scrambled to my feet again—scared to death.

I got past the bandstand. Ahead of me was the little red brick building. I could see now that it was a public toilet. If I could just get in there and close the door!

My knee was hurting me, but I was paying no attention to that. My chest was heaving and I was huffing and puffing and constantly looking over my shoulder. You'll never know how happy I was when I reached that door with L-A-D-I-E-S painted on it.

In an instant, I was inside, leaning against the closed door, panting and wondering what I must do next.

The man might be lame, all right, but he was much stronger than I was and he could force the door in mighty short order.

High on the far wall was a window that let in enough of the failing light so that I could see what was there. Well, there wasn't much—two stalls, two basins, and a big mirror with most of the silver gone, a rickety old chair, and a large plastic garbage can under the paper-towel dispenser. I thought maybe I could prop the chair under the doorknob. But the back of the chair looked like it was ready to come off.

Then I thought of my revolver. What a smart thing it was to have brought that revolver! I looked down at the purse hanging from my arm. My purse was open.

And the revolver—was not there. It was back at that confounded rabbit hole!

All for the want of a horseshoe nail!

It's the little things that betray us. Why had I not had presence of mind enough to check on that revolver when I struggled to my feet and began to run again?

By this time, I could hear the man outside. He stopped at the door. Then I heard him walking back and forth, and it occurred to me that he, the same as I, was trying to decide what he would do next. Poor man! He was only trying to protect his daughter—but I can't explain that now.

Well, thank God the man was hesitant for just that little time. It gave me a moment to think what I would do. And right away I saw how to do it.

I put the chair so that it would be more or less hidden until the man opened the door all the way. Then I emptied the wadded-up paper towels out of the plastic garbage can.

As for the next part, I'm glad there was nobody there to see me. Because I climbed up on that wobbly old chair, and, being wobbly myself, I must have been quite a spectacle. But no matter!

Anyhow, I got up there and got hold of the plastic garbage can and lifted it up and waited for the man outside to make up his mind to come through that door.

Finally, he did. First, he pushed the door open a little bit—very timidly—and looked in. Then he pushed the door open farther and was already inside before he knew where I was. Because, you know, it was fairly dark in there.

Then he took a little step toward me, and I had him.

I brought that plastic garbage can down over his head and pressed on it with all my might. Being somewhat flexible, the garbage can came down neatly over his shoulders, down past his elbows, pinning them tightly against his side. In fact, the garbage can came down over his great big belly and made a very snug fit, thank you.

I could hear muffled noises coming through the plastic and

the garbage can was gyrating about in a very energetic way, but he would not be able to get it off very easily without help.

I'm afraid I laughed at the poor man.

Well, I was in a most unusual situation. The man was my prisoner, but I was at a loss to know how to keep him that way. I couldn't just go off and leave him. Sooner or later, he would wiggle free of the garbage can and get away if I didn't prevent it.

While he was threshing around—couldn't see anything, you know—I got down off that old chair, stepped around my prisoner, gave him just a little push out of the way, went outside, and closed the door.

The door was sort of ramshackle and not at all strong. Someone had put a hasp-and-staple arrangement on it—maybe to keep transients out of it at night—there was no padlock now. But if I could jam something through the staple, that would hold my prisoner until I could get the police.

I was trying to figure out what on earth to do, when who should show up with his rifle but Robert Smith!

"Bless Patsy!" I said. "How did you get here?"

"My grandmother told me to come and keep an eye on you."

The dear boy had been hidden behind the bleachers on the baseball field. He had been expecting me to come from the other side of the park and had not spotted me or my assailant until that man pushed open the rest room door. Then Robert had come on the run.

It was just wonderful. I felt like Daniel delivered from the lion's den. Everything was working out perfectly. Mr. Brazille was in the ladies' room, where he shouldn't be; and when the police came, there was no way he could pretend he hadn't been about to—kidnap me?—attack me?—kill me? Anyway, he had "attempted" something and the police ought to be able to bring some kind of charge against him.

If they could find his old van hidden out there somewhere in the weeds and the bushes, and if there was a cut in the right rear tire, and if the tire matched the track that was found after my dear old DeSoto was blown up—if all those things—and I was pretty sure the van would be there and the tire would be the one that made the track—well, in that case—don't you see—I had him.

And if he *was* Mr. Brazille, as I had no doubt he was, then that daughter of his would have to explain a lot. But more about that later.

"Robert," I said, "let me have your rifle, and I'll stay here while you go and call the police."

He didn't argue. He handed over the rifle, and skedaddled. As soon as he got away, I slipped the muzzle of the rifle through the staple, effectively locking Brazille in the rest room. Thank goodness the thing didn't go off, for I certainly did not wish to endanger poor Mr. Brazille's life. I wanted him for evidence. And no matter how undignified my use of Robert's rifle may have been, it did its job just fine.

In about ten minutes, I heard the police siren—such a beautiful sound! I never before appreciated it properly.

Well, the police took Mr. Brazille in for questioning. I don't think he was at all happy about it. They put him in the police car. As soon as I recovered my revolver, I got into my car and followed them down to the police station, while Robert came along after me.

At the station, I made a preliminary statement, and while I was talking to the chief, one of the officers came in and said they had found the van and that the tire had a cut just like the track they had found after my old DeSoto was destroyed.

"Well," the chief said to me, "you certainly caught your man."

"Robert helped me," I insisted. "He saved my life." And I patted the boy on the shoulder and embarrassed him.

They said I would have to talk with the district attorney the following day. They also said I would have to be a witness and testify in court there in Stedbury. Poor Maud would have me for a houseguest for quite a while in that case.

Maud!

I hadn't thought about her. She would be beside herself thinking something awful had happened to me—and even worse—to Robert! So I called her and let her know it was all right and made Robert call his parents.

Then a reporter came in and interviewed us and took a picture of Robert and me.

It was 10:30 before I got back to Maud's house. I don't know when I've been so tired, and my knee was hurting. I soaked in a lovely tub of hot water, went to bed, and slept the sleep of the just—even if I didn't deserve it.

HARRIET'S REPORT

>> Henry Delaporte <<

It was about 2:30. The afternoon was hot. Cindi informed me that a Mrs. Bushrow was on the line.

"Mr. Delaporte," her commanding voice announced, "I need to see you at your earliest convenience."

"Why? Has something happened?" I asked.

"Indeed something has. But I didn't realize how complicated it was going to be. So I need your help."

"Certainly," I said. "I can see you now if you please."

When she arrived, I observed immediately that she had not dressed with her usual care. She had business to attend to and was in no mood to engage in unnecessary pleasantries.

Once she was seated in my office, she gave a voluble account of her experiences of the two preceding days. Very clearly, she pointed out the problem. A Mr. Brazille was being held in Stedbury for offenses committed in North Carolina. In order to bring the murderer of Charles Hollonbrook to justice for the crime committed in Virginia, it would be necessary to get certain information from Brazille. From the North Carolina point of view, they had nothing tangible to link Brazille to a murder that Virginia was perfectly willing to call a suicide. Could she convince the Commonwealth Attorney to reopen the case and reverse the Virginia finding of suicide? She thought she could, and she felt that the murderer and her accomplice would escape if action were not taken quickly.

I asked her how she expected to convince the Commonwealth Attorney. She told me how. I agreed to call Ron Jefferson and did so.

"I have Mrs. Bushrow in my office," I said. "She has information that indicates that Charles Hollonbrook was murdered. You remember—Hollonbrook, the one who turned up dead at the Borderville Inn a month ago." There was a pause.

The reader may remember that in the Famous DAR Murder Mystery, Mrs. Bushrow and the other ladies of the DAR made the Commonwealth Attorney out to be such a fool that no one connected with law enforcement on either side of the state line would dare refuse Harriet Bushrow a hearing.

"Oh yes, Mrs. Bushrow!"

"She would like to have a conference with you at the Inn as soon as possible." I looked over at Mrs. B. as if to ask, Is that right?

"Can't she come to my office?"

I covered the mouthpiece of the phone and repeated the CA's question. Mrs. B. was negative.

"Ron, I think Mrs. Bushrow wants to demonstrate something and can only do so at the Inn."

By this time, Ron had decided it would be to his advantage to accede to Mrs. Bushrow's demands sooner rather than later, and at 4:15 the three of us were seated around one of the poolside tables at the Borderville Inn, with glasses of iced tea before us.

Mrs. Bushrow began to explain.

"Mr. Jefferson, I appreciate your finding time to listen to my story so promptly, as I am sure you will find that unless something is done immediately the murderer, who has already fled, will be very difficult to find. I believe you people in the law say that 'the trail grows cold' in cases like this, don't you?

"Well, I'll just begin at the beginning, because that's the only way you can get the whole picture.

"Charles Hollonbrook was a boy from a small town in south-side Virginia. He was smart but unsophisticated. At Granville State College, he was taken into a fraternity on account of his grades. I have no doubt that he felt socially inferior to the other boys. And as so often happens, he began to pick up on their ways without being able to see those things in perspective.

"Of course, that was at the time of the Vietnam War. So Charles went into the service, was commissioned, and received several medals for bravery before he was injured and given an honorable discharge.

"He got over his injury, married, and took up the real estate business in Stedbury, North Carolina.

"The same drive that had brought him success in the army pushed him right along in the real estate business. He made a small killing when he brought Featherstone Plastics to Stedbury and received a good deal of recognition in the community, too.

"He liked this, and he began to travel with a little better class of society. Unfortunately, his wife did not climb the ladder as easily as he did.

"I have no doubt that Charles had had experience with women at college and in the army; and now, since he was dissatisfied with his wife and happened to have a very attractive and intelligent secretary, he began an affair with her.

"After his divorce, he married his secretary, Alice, who was to serve as an ornament to his social progress. He joined the country club and the Episcopal church. Alice learned quickly and filled her role easily and well.

"Charles had a fling with the wife of the golf pro at the club—apparently an attractive little piece of fluff. That was about 1981. The affair was not serious on Hollonbrook's part, but his wife, Alice, was undoubtedly more upset by the affair than she admitted to me. However that may be, Charles took out a policy for half a million on his life, with Alice as beneficiary—undoubtedly in his mind some kind of reparation to Alice for his affair with Desiree Patterson, the golf pro's wife. But at the same time, that life-insurance policy made it possible for him to have his flings from time to time with impunity, since Alice would lose the prospect of a half million dollars if she should divorce him.

"Meanwhile, Charles had gotten himself another secretary. This one was a most unlikely person, a Miss Paula Stout.

"Now she is not stout—in fact, she is pleasantly plump. Her problem is that she is not pretty.

"That can be a great concern to a young girl—specially if she has a beautiful sister such as Paula had. People are always saying unkind things in a situation like that—commenting on the pretty child and saying nothing about the other. And, of course, the pretty sister has numbers of boyfriends, while the other has none.

"Poor Paula took refuge in being 'good' if she could not be beautiful—not because she liked being good, understand, but because she thought she could be appreciated in that way. Unfortunately, people don't often appreciate goodness as much as they do beauty.

"However, Paula had other talents besides 'goodness.' She was dependable—necessary for the orderly function of the office—and ready to do anything for her employer—even feeding the dog when both Hollonbrooks were away from home.

"She was something more than a doormat, but there was part of her personality that she kept wisely hidden.

"It may seem strange that Charles Hollonbrook should become sexually attracted to Paula Stout. Beauty is clearly a strong attribute when sexual attraction is concerned. But there is other magnetism, and availability is a great part of it.

"I don't know just how it happened. Oh, maybe one day a

certain paper couldn't immediately be found. Perhaps he was looking over her shoulder as she was searching in the file case. Then as she turned around, she was in his arms. The girl who had never been kissed had thought about it a great deal. And in one unexpected embrace, Charles Hollonbrook may have learned that desire was burning in the breast of that little do-gooder, Paula Stout.

"From an episode like that, given the proclivities of Charles Hollonbrook and the psychological needs of Paula Stout, it would be only a short time before Paula was her employer's mistress.

"I don't suppose the girl felt any guilt about it at all. You see, she had been a hypocrite most of her life. It probably gave her pleasure secretly to be a scarlet woman while everyone thought she was a saint, to deceive the world that had been so cruel to her.

"So Charles was having the best of it with the beautiful, socially accepted mistress of his household—and Paula, mistress of his office, feeding his ego and his sexual appetite with a passion he no longer received from his wife.

"Now how long could that go on? Sooner or later, Paula was going to ask herself why she should not be acknowledged to the world. In short, the time must have come when Paula saw that her romance wasn't getting her anywhere. I feel sure she demanded that Charles divorce Alice.

Divorce Alice and marry Paula? Alice was beautiful. Divorce Alice and marry a woman who though not ugly was obviously plain? Not only that, she had a reputation for being plain. And besides, people who join the Episcopal church for social reasons don't divorce an Episcopalian and marry a Baptist. People would talk about it, and Charles would look silly. I fancy marriage with Paula was not for Charles Hollonbrook.

"He solved his problem in 1985 by taking out a policy on his life for half a million, payable to Paula Stout. The technique had worked very well in pacifying Alice Hollonbrook, and it operated on Paula Stout in the same way.

"All went well until recently, when something good and something bad happened to Charles Hollonbrook. When the real estate market fell off, he realized he had overextended himself. That was the bad thing. The good thing was that he was president of the Stedbury Rotary Club and—marvel of marvels—district governor–elect for the following year. For Charles, as it would be for anyone, that was very good indeed.

"Being district governor is just like being on the vestry of the Episcopal church and belonging to the country club. If it is for the right reasons, it is very good. But if the reasons are wrong, you had better leave it alone.

"Well, I won't say that is beside the point, because it is very much to the point. All the same, it does lead away from the story. So, to get on the track again—

"An attractive widow—grass widow, that is—came back to town. Kimberlin Mayburn—beautiful, rich, aristocratic, and charming. She had a past—married to a Frenchman—and what's more, a dissolute Frenchman with a passion for boys.

"Now, no matter how modern we may be about homosexuals, almost everybody condemns involving children in something like that. And to think of poor Kim married to a man—and a Frenchman at that—who runs off with boys! Well, you can see how Charles could glow with masculine tenderness at the thought of consoling the poor girl, who has position, sophistication—and money, which he is going to need pretty soon.

"Well, last February Charles Hollonbrook took out a policy on his life for half a million, payable to Kimberlin Mayburn. Apparently, as a side effect, taking out sizable policies on his life gave a boost to his ego. But then, who can explain what goes on in some people's minds?

"The new policy in itself was not necessarily the death warrant for Charles Hollonbrook. The thing that did it was that he canceled the policy that would have been paid to Paula. He did not altogether burn his bridges behind him, you see, because he left Alice's policy in effect. Perhaps he wasn't sure of hooking Kim and wanted to keep Alice in his creel.

"There was something about Paula that Charles either did not know or neglected to think about. Paula had a crony, a bosom friend, also one of life's rejects, Nellie Penn, very much in the same mold as Paula, even less attractive, and also a Baptist.

"Now I have a great advantage here in that my friend Maud Bradfield is an active member of the First Baptist Church of Stedbury, North Carolina. And in addition to that, her late husband had the Bradfield Agency—life insurance, you see. And Maud has her ways of finding out what she wants to know.

"It doesn't take much feminine intuition to conclude that Nellie told Paula that her policy had been canceled or that, in a way of speaking, it had been transferred to Kim."

At this point, Mrs. Bushrow paused. It was evident that our Commonwealth Attorney did not have feminine intuition and consequently did not make the desired conclusion, and Mrs. Bushrow saw it in his face.

"Just wait," she said. "When I get through with this, you'll see that it just had to be."

Then she continued: "Paula was furious. Of course she did not let on to Charles. But from that moment, she began to plot revenge.

"Meanwhile, what about Alice? Paula didn't mind too much about Alice, but for Kim to receive half a million in life insurance that ought to go to Paula—well, that was entirely too much for Paula!

"That's where it became important that Charles was now district governor and would have to go around to visit all the clubs in his district.

"Because, you see, Paula Stout made all the arrangements for his visits. She knew that he would be in Ambrose Courthouse for an evening club on the twenty-sixth of May and Borderville for a meeting here at a noon club on the twenty-seventh. And she had a secret weapon, which I'll tell you about in a little while.

"Now Mrs. Alice Hollonbrook, left to her own devices as you might say, and put out to grass with the prospect of a half-million-dollar life-insurance policy, had made her own arrangements. These had been going on for some time, and Paula Stout could count on them. When Charles went out of town for any reason, Alice also left town to be with a gentleman who seemed to appreciate her more than Charles did. It was just a regular thing that when both Charles and Alice Hollonbrook went out of town, Paula Stout had a key to the house so she could feed the dog.

"So, when Alice took advantage of her husband's absence to spend some time with her light of love on his yacht, Paula took advantage of Alice's absence to gather the things she needed for her plan.

"Paula was aware—the fact is, the whole town of Stedbury knew—that Charles Hollonbrook had a pistol range in the basement of his house, where he practiced. Paula also knew that Alice made him use a silencer.

"So all Paula had to do was take the key that had been given her, go into the house, enter the bedroom, where Charles had no doubt taken her a number of times before. The key to the drawer where Charles kept his pistols, silencer, and ammunition was right there in his dresser.

"And as for the so-called suicide note, it may possibly have been written to Paula. We'll never know the true situation involved, for you know the note said: 'Sorry to disappoint you, but I can't make it today.' The note could have been meant for the gun-club members, but just suppose that it was calling off an assignation with Paula, and suppose the reason why he was calling it off was that he was having an assignation with his new ladylove, Kimberlin Mayburn. If Paula had had any suspicion of such a thing, it would have made her absolutely furious.

"She would be determined on revenge and such a revenge as would rob Kim Mayburn of her half million. As far as Alice's half million went, Paula didn't care about that. Charles in effect had left Alice for Paula—and he had signed, sealed, and delivered his endorsement of Paula's position with that life-insurance policy, which he had now canceled. To be sure, the premiums were expensive, and he had money problems. But all the same, it was a mistake to cancel Paula's policy.

"So Charles was to die by 'suicide' and Paula would be even with both Charles and Kim."

Ron Jefferson was looking at Mrs. B. with his mouth open. At that point, I didn't think he was at all convinced, but he was certainly drawn into her account.

"Don't tell me women don't react that way," she said. "I am eighty-eight years old, and I've never been anything but a woman since I was a girl."

She bestowed a beaming smile on both of us.

"Now," she said as she picked up her purse and rose from the table, "let's go to this room over here and I'll show you how Paula Stout 'committed suicide' on Charles Hollonbrook in a locked room."

I had arranged that a room would be available for Mrs. Bushrow's demonstration, and Nancy Attwood, the manager of the Inn, had been standing at the door of room 112 for some minutes, waiting for us.

Mrs. Bushrow led us like a conquering general. She smiled sweetly and bowed slightly to Mrs. Attwood, who appeared as curious as I myself was to see how the trick was to be done.

We all entered the room.

Mrs. Bushrow said, "Now which of you gentlemen wishes to act the part of Charles Hollonbrook?"

I volunteered.

"Very well," she continued, "you got here no later than nine-thirty on that Monday evening because the evening club in Ambrose Courthouse would be done by seven-thirty and then you would have been served a drink with the president of the Ambrose club and would have come down here.

"You had a book with you—a good book by Mr. Dick Francis. So you got into bed and enjoyed your book until eleven-thirty, which is the time you usually go to sleep unless you have other entertainment. You take a sleeping pill because, as your wife attests, you always take a sleeping pill when you stay at a motel. You say it helps you sleep through the noise of late arrivals and early departures.

"So it is beddy-bye, and you sleep soundly—well, I guess you sleep soundly for the rest of your life, because around two o'clock, when she knows from experience you will be snoring away, your 'office' mistress in gloves and running shoes, or whatever, comes silently, silently into the room with her flashlight and *your* pistol with *your* silencer on it. She has brought along the note, with which she perhaps thinks you rejected her for someone else; and she is about to make sure that the half million that you intended for her rival will never be paid.

"She holds the gun in the position that you would have to hold it in to blow your own brains out. She pulls the trigger; the gun discharges. She places the gun in your right hand to add fresh fingerprints to the other prints that are already there— your prints, because she has worn gloves whenever she handled the gun, the silencer, and the ammunition.

"Paula lays the 'suicide' note on the nightstand and silently leaves the room."

It is a pity Mrs. B. never tried for a career on the stage. We were entranced by her recreation of the murder. But Ron Jefferson broke the spell.

"That's very good except for four things that destroy your whole theory. First, the key to the room was inside the room when the body was found. Second, a silencer is not perfect. People in the adjoining rooms and the room above would have heard. Third, even if the 'murderer' had a key to the room, she could not know that the chain would not be on the door when she wished to enter. And fourth, you have not explained how the chain could be on the door when the body was found."

"Ah," said Mrs. Bushrow, delighted that the Commonwealth Attorney had fallen into her trap. "You do not realize that Paula Stout had a secret weapon. The young lady who worked here until recently—Miss Teddy Brazille—was Paula Stout's niece, and that made all the difference.

"You perhaps recall that Paula had a beautiful sister. Teddy is the daughter of that sister. 'Beautiful mother—more beautiful daughter.' Why should a beautiful girl want to waste her life as a room clerk in a motel? Is there not a career for her? Is there not New York? She longs to be a glamorous model, and her aunt has promised to supply her with money to go to a school that will guarantee all the instruction that it takes to wear beautiful clothes and prance around in front of department-store buyers and whatnot.

"All Teddy has to do is assign the rooms on May 26 in such a way that nobody is placed in the rooms above and on either side of Charles Hollonbrook. That's not such a wicked thing, is it? And she must give her aunt a pass key when she arrives. After all, the aunt has been in motels with her lover before. And then the other thing . . ."

Once more, Mrs. Bushrow rummaged in her purse, and this time came up with a Phillips screwdriver.

"Dollar twenty-five at Ace Hardware," she said, holding it up. "Here's the other thing she had to do." Mrs. Bushrow began removing the linkage mechanism. "She simply took this thing off before Hollonbrook got here. A man is not nervous about someone coming into his room in the middle of the night. One lock would certainly be enough for Charles Hollonbrook, a war hero and all. And so, with the door locked behind him the last time he came into the room, he laid his key on the bedside table, where it remained until the room was broken into the next day."

"And now for how the chain got back on the door, you are

going to have to stay in here while the rest of us go outside, or else the motel people will have to break into a 'locked room,' " she said to me.

"Oh no you don't," I said. "I want to see how you do this."

She smiled. "How very ungallant of you, Mr. Delaporte! For poor Mrs. Attwood will have to stay if you go out with us."

Mrs. Attwood agreed to remain, and Mrs. Bushrow continued.

"Very well, Mrs. Attwood, please give me your key." Mrs. Attwood surrendered the key. Mrs. Bushrow gave it to me, saying, "Here, hold this."

She was opening her purse and rummaging. At last, she found what she wanted: a heavy black thread.

She held it up for us to see. "Clark's ONT, number eight. Use it for sewing on overcoat buttons."

Then she pointed to the arrangement for securing the door on the inside. It was not the old-fashioned chain, but it served the same purpose. It was a link of metal attached by a swivel to the inner side of the door in such a way that when the door was closed, the link could be thrust over a hook attached to the doorjamb.

Mrs. Bushrow ushered us out of the room. Being careful that we could see what she was doing, she looped her thread over the link. Then, holding the ends of the thread in one hand, she closed the door with the other. With a gentle pull from the outside of the door, she propelled the link inside the door over the hook, where it would remain until someone inside the room disengaged the link.

Dropping one end of the thread, she pulled the whole of it free of the door and handed it to me. Receiving the key from me, she inserted it in the lock, turned it, and removed it again.

"Take the key, Mr. Commonwealth Attorney," she said, handing it to him, "and see if you can get in."

Ron said, "I'll be damned."

"Go ahead, unlock the door," she urged.

Ron inserted the key, turned it in the lock, and pushed the door open as far as it would go—about three-quarters of an inch.

"I think you had better open the door for us, Mrs. Attwood." Mrs. B. had raised her voice slightly.

Mrs. Attwood closed the door, disengaged the mechanism, and opened the door again.

Mrs. Bushrow had very effectively knocked the wind out of Ron Jefferson's sails.

"And now," she said, "I think we had better go back to our nice table by the pool so I can tell you what you must do."

Ron followed her like a little boy being conducted by his mother at a wedding reception.

"Now," she began, when we were seated, "you are no doubt wondering what proof I have of all this. I haven't any, but I'm going to tell you how *you* can get proof.

"It's *my* 'secret weapon,' you see.

"When I began to look into all of this—after these gentlemen in the Rotary Club asked me to do it—I had no idea of this 'secret weapon.' If I had known who Teddy Brazille was, I would have known the whole thing right away. But I didn't know, and I went over there to Stedbury and stayed with my friend Maud and flounced around and poked my nose into everybody's business. And in short order, I had warned every possible suspect that there was a determined old woman rooting around in their dirty linen.

"Nobody likes a busybody. You know that. But when my car was blown up, I knew I had gotten very close to 'who done it.' "

Jefferson did not know about the bombing of the DeSoto and Mrs. B. explained it in some detail before getting back to her purpose.

"When I found—by accident—right here at the Inn that Teddy had come into a lot of money, I realized that she was an accomplice. She probably was not as bright as she might be and, I tried to think, perhaps not fully conscious of what she was doing. And who could the man with that blasting gelatin be?

"Now I knew that Paula Stout was Teddy's aunt. So I went snooping about in Stedbury again, and of course everybody in that little town knew what I was up to. The librarian had recognized me on the first day, and after that I might as well have been on television. And I knew that whoever had dynamited my car would have to attack me again.

"Well, the long and short of it is that if he hasn't been bailed out, poor Mr. Brazille is over there in the Stedbury jail on a charge of blowing up my car. You see, he is the key to my evidence."

This last was directed significantly to Ron Jefferson.

"Mr. Commonwealth Attorney, you can work with the authorities down there in North Carolina. Get them to drop the charges against Mr. Brazille, or agree to a minor sentence or probation if he will cooperate with us against Paula Stout."

"But, Mrs. Bushrow," Jefferson objected, "does he have any positive evidence against the Stout woman?"

"Perhaps not, but Teddy Brazille does. And if you can find her, you can cut the same deal with her: If she and her father tell what they know, charges against both will be dropped, light sentences imposed, or probation granted.

"At this point, Mr. Brazille can't have much love for Paula Stout. I have no doubt the father will lean on the daughter, especially if both of them can get off without a heavy sentence.

"Now, Mr. Jefferson, I know you are a smart man and can figure all those little negotiations out.

"I'll tell you one thing. I bet the father knows where the girl is."

"I see what you mean," Ron replied. He exchanged a few blandishments with Mrs. Bushrow and left—in fact, to take action on the lady's suggestion.

LAST CHAPTER

>> Harriet Bushrow <<

Professor Landrum says that Plato or Aristotle—or one of those old Greek philosophers—said that a story had to have a beginning, a middle, and an end. Well, what is an end? Don't you just stop? No, no, says Professor Landrum, the end must tie up all the loose threads and tell the reader what happened to all the people he has met in the story.

Now don't you like that idea? Because, you see, Henry Delaporte left the whole thing hanging in the last chapter. He didn't say anything about the trial and how it all turned out. I said to him, "Henry Delaporte, you are the lawyer and you must write it up," because, for me at least, it was the best part.

Well, he said it would just be a repetition of what the reader already knows, and maybe he was right. Anyhow, I'll brush over it lightly.

Mr. Jefferson did just what I told him to, and both Mr. Brazille and Teddy agreed to be witnesses for the prosecution. As I predicted, Paula Stout tried to run away. But when her money ran out, she was picked up for forgery. She didn't know how to do it, you see. And so there was another charge against her.

I don't know how she had the nerve, but Paula pleaded

innocent. She was counting on her alibi, poor girl! That old fool Rose Moody admitted on the witness stand that she couldn't hear a thing without her hearing aid. Oh yes, she said, she always took it out of her ear before she went to bed; and, yes indeed, that sweet Paula had brought her a nice glass of warm milk before she retired for the night on May 26. Could there have been sleeping medicine in it? She *did* think she *had* slept rather well.

So that did away with Paula's alibi, because it takes less than two hours to drive from Stedbury to Borderville and no time at all to kill Charles Hollonbrook. Then two hours back to Stedbury. There was no alibi left at all.

They had me on the stand, you know. I had to explain how Paula could make it look like the room was locked. And when Maud heard I was going to testify, she had Robert drive her up to Borderville. They stayed with me. And Robert enjoyed the trial, too, because of his part in rescuing me from the "foul clutches" of poor Mr. Brazille.

Paula got a life sentence, but I suppose she'll be out in five years or so.

Alice Hollonbrook collected her half million in insurance money, but I am afraid she was right about the estate itself. Now that Estonia Savings and Loan's president was free of blackmail, he was able to foreclose on the Hollonbrook property. And though I understand that his business is in pretty shaky condition, they say that there is a chance he will pull through since real estate is looking up a little.

And Vic Douglass, the fraternity brother of Charles Hollonbrook—you remember how Hollonbrook cheated him when Featherstone Plastics came to Stedbury—well, that sweet, dear boy wants to bring Alice Hollonbrook into his real estate firm. The two of them have an offer to act as agents in disposing of the Hollondale property for Estonia Savings. In her last letter, Alice was seriously thinking about taking Vic up on his proposal.

After the foreclosure, there was hardly enough of the Hollonbrook estate left to divide. So it looked as though the children were going to have to find the money for college somewhere else—until that sweet, dear Alice Hollonbrook offered to pay their expenses at Estonia State. I prophesy that Alice won't be much out-of-pocket, for I can't imagine any one of those children in college for longer than a few months.

Poor Kim Mayburn! I'm afraid she is completely "around the bend." They had to put her in a private sanitarium. At least she got her half million from the insurance. With that and the money she already had, she can afford to be crazy. The rest of us just have to go on and hope nobody will notice.

Teddy Brazille pleaded guilty, of course. They couldn't just drop the charges as if nothing had happened, but in return for her testimony against her aunt, she drew a ten-year suspended sentence. She is still trying to be a model. She's such a beautiful girl; I hate to see her ruin her life. But she thinks she'll never get old, and it takes so much character for a girl not to have her head turned by something as glamorous as modeling.

Mr. Brazille! In spite of what he did, I kind of liked him. He was not prosecuted because I did not press charges against him after he agreed to testify against Paula. When Paula's verdict came in, he came to me and apologized—said he knew what he'd done was wrong, but Paula had put him up to it—told him if he couldn't frighten me into silence, his girl would go to jail. Well, who can blame a man for protecting his daughter? Besides, the poor old man is probably none too smart.

And since you already know that Buck Patterson—the golf pro, you remember—is back with his wife, that just about takes care of everyone.

Oh—I was about to forget.

The Rotary Foundation has this wonderful Paul Harris Fellowship. It does such marvelous things. It's their agency that has just about stamped out polio the whole world over. To be a Paul Harris Fellow, someone has to pay one thousand dollars. That's how they get the money to do those wonderful things.

Well at their banquet in October, who do you suppose that wonderful Rotary Club gave one of those Paul Harris Fellowships to?

Me!